the dogs of pompeii

© 2010 Barry Creyton & Vaughan Edwards

Cinelit Management

cinelit@att.net

www.dogsofpompeii.com

Copyright © 2010 Vaughan Edwards & Barry Creyton
All rights reserved.

ISBN: 1453859519
ISBN-13: 9781453859513
Library of Congress Control Number: 2010914998

Acknowledgements

The authors wish to thank their friend,
Dr Franco Bruni of the French Institute
of History and Archaeology in Rome
for his assistance.

*

Cover illustrations by Benjamin Fretwell

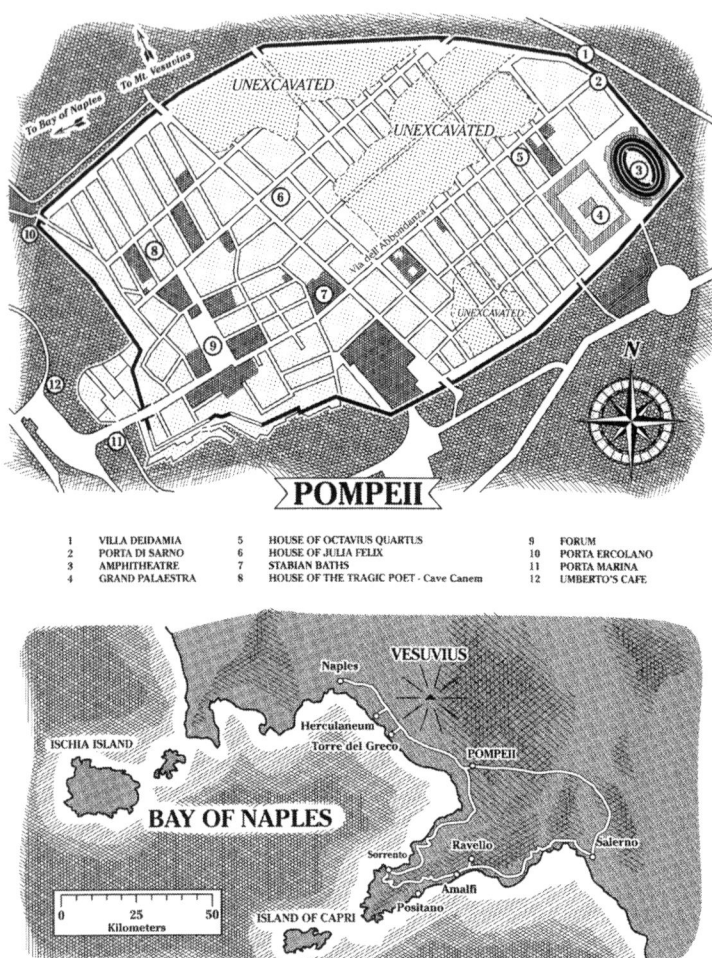

Map of Pompeii and Amalfi Coast by
Dylan J. Hay Chapman

CHAPTER 1

FROM THE UNPUBLISHED MEMOIRS OF NERO NERONE

(dictated not read)

Most mornings when you wake up, you pretty much know what the day will bring. Before you fall asleep, you go over what you hope to achieve, mentally check off chores to be done, maybe decide what you'll have for breakfast. Just another day, you think. And most days you'd be right.

But one morning last July, the life I'd always known ended and a completely new one took its place.

I've always been a bit of a loner, never knew my folks. When I was three days old, I was found on the doorstep of Umberto's, a little sidewalk cafe just outside the ancient ruined city of Pompeii, Italy. Pompeii is now a mega tourist trap, but that's okay – keep the economy moving, I say. It trickles down and benefits the locals, like me.

I never had what you'd call a formal education – it was mostly at the hands of Fiammetta, Signor Umberto's cook. She wasn't much of a teacher, but she did give me an appreciation of her two great passions in life – food and television.

She liked old movies – really old movies. One Christmas, Signor Umberto gave her a DVD player and she stocked up on all the classics. Her favorite was a good one – 'Casablanca'. We watched it over and over. That movie's got everything – history, romance, suspense – and Humphrey Bogart. Maybe you never heard of him, but he was a famous movie star way back when. A tough guy, with a sensitive streak.

He became my role model. I spent hours copying his walk and his attitude. I even started talking out of the side of my mouth for anyone who'd listen. But I never thought my life would be as dramatic as his – until the day I met Caroline.

I was up early that day, woken by a garbage truck in the alley behind Umberto's, which is usually quiet until the garbage guys start slinging their cans around. I closed my eyes and tried to get back into a dream where I was the only guest at a sit-down dinner for thirty, but it was impossible. I sat up, got both eyes operating more or less in sync and thought about breakfast.

I always have breakfast at Umberto's. It's not the Ritz, but it's close to home, and most days you run into someone who's willing to spring for a meal in exchange for a little civilized company. Tourists weren't out yet and only a couple of tables were occupied: one by a group of construction workers; the other by someone I'd never seen before – a sinister looking guy in a black suit. A black eye patch covered one of his eyes, and an ugly white scar stretched from under the patch down to his jaw. He didn't look like he was enjoying his breakfast. Come to that, he didn't look like he enjoyed anything much.

Tony, my waiter buddy, was getting tables set up while his sidekick Vittorio hosed down the sidewalk. I skirted round him to avoid getting wet. In my line of work appearance is everything.

Tony gave me a wink. "Ciao, amico. What's up?"

I tried to smile. Doesn't do to bite the hand that feeds you.

"Boss ain't in the best mood this morning. Maybe you should come back later."

I took the hint. Last thing I needed was a run-in with Signor Umberto on an empty stomach. I decided to go across the street until the tour buses started showing up. There's a nice shady spot under the umbrella pines where nobody bothers you.

Tony gave me a wave. "Later, Nero."

Okay, I know what you're thinking and I don't have an answer for you. Why a decent, law-abiding individual like me should end up named after the craziest, most notorious of all Roman emperors is beyond me. It's not the name I was born with, but try telling my friends that. I've been Nero as long as I can remember and there's not much I can do about it.

It was nice and cool under the trees and I was just thinking I might skip breakfast and catch up on some of that lost sleep and – that's when I saw her.

Of all the gin joints in all the towns in all the world, she'd walked into mine. I'm not too sure what a gin joint is, but one thing was for sure, she was the prettiest girl I'd ever laid eyes on!

She was sitting at a sidewalk table. She wore shorts, a pretty shirt and a big straw hat. Her hair was fair and cascaded down to her shoulders and there was a sprinkling of freckles on an open, generous face.

Who was she? Not a local – I would have recognized

her. Not Italian – she wasn't on a mobile phone. English? Didn't have the attitude... you know, complaining the tea's not right and calling you a foreigner. I always want to say, "Hey, lady, *you're* the foreigner. I *live* here!" But back to the story.

She smiled. "Caffè latte, per favore, e una frittata al formaggio." The accent was a dead giveaway: American. Of course! I love Americans! I've been known to benefit from their generosity for weeks at a stretch. She took off her sunglasses and opened a book. An intellectual! Okay by me. I love good conversation.

Tony brought her coffee and a pastry and went back inside. The coast was clear, if only Signor Umberto would stay out of the way for a while. I started back across the street to the café.

She glanced my way. "Well, hi! Or should I say buon giorno?" That warm smile again. I did my best to smile back. "My name's Caroline" she said. "Won't you sit down?"

This was almost too easy. Someone tells me to sit, I sit. I sat. She sighed blissfully and stretched her legs. "Isn't it a beautiful day?"

Okay, I know the dialogue here isn't brilliant, but her Italian wasn't great, and mine – well, the less said the better. But things were going pretty well. That is, until Tony showed up with a fully loaded tray balanced on his shoulder.

Did I mention I have this talent for being in the wrong place at the wrong time?

I've no idea how it happened, but next thing I knew, Tony's tray was flying through the air and plates of food were bouncing off the walls. The construction workers thought it was hilarious until they realized it was their breakfast that was decorating the sidewalk – and Caroline.

She tried to put a good face on it, but I could tell she wasn't pleased. Tony struggled to his feet. Now, he and I go way back, but for a minute I really thought he was going to kill me. Suddenly everyone was looking at me like it was all my fault! I thought it best to cut my losses and exit with dignity.

That's when Signor Umberto showed up.

Signor Umberto – how can I describe him? Think Don Vito Corleone in 'The Godfather', or Stromboli in 'Pinocchio' – without the charm. Now it was Stromboli, right down to the smoke pouring out of his ears.

"Signorina, scusi, scusi! Sono molto, molto spiacente!" He was weeping copiously and babbling apologies right in Caroline's face, which must have been about as welcome as the plate of eggs down her front.

Forget dignity. I just had to get out of there. Unfortunately, I didn't make it before the sinister guy with the scar and the eye-patch caught up with me. He landed me a kick in the butt that took me out onto the street – right into the path of a passing motor scooter!

CHAPTER 2

CAROLINE DONOHUE'S JOURNAL

Pensione Excelsior
Via Villa dei Misteri 16
80045 Pompeii-Scavi
Sunday, July 10

When Dad asked me what I wanted for my fifteenth birthday, without even thinking about it I said, 'Italy!' and he gave me that in-your-dreams look, like when Kevin asks to borrow the Beamer. Kevin's my older brother. When he was born, Grandpa said, "Kevin? What kind of name is that? Give the kid a good Italian name like his grandfather!" Sanity prevailed, I'm happy to say. Can you imagine going through high school with a brother called Antonio Donohue? My best friend Didi Carr says, "An Irish father and Italian mother – how cool is that?" But what it comes down to is that I've got Dad's freckles and, if I don't lay off the junk food, Mom's butt.

Anyway, Mom and Dad locked themselves in the den for what seemed like days and when they came out Mom said she'd email Uncle Tad. He's her big brother, Taddeo Garibaldi, Professor of Archaeology at Naples University and Director of Excavations at Pompeii (I *think* I've got that right). So after Mom and Uncle Tad exchanged about three million emails it was decided I'd spend my summer break in Pompeii, working as a sort of unofficial assistant on his new dig. Actually what I had in mind was something more like cruising the streets of Rome in a white Ferrari, or water-skiing down the Grand Canal. I don't think they allow water-skiing on the Grand Canal, but you know what I mean. Still, it *is* Italy and I'm somewhere on my own for the first time in my life.

I've never kept a journal before, but it's one of Dad's conditions of the trip, so he and Mom presented me with an iPad – an early xmas present they said, so don't expect anything from them come December! It's super slim, with all the bells and whistles like an attachable keyboard, great for traveling, for storing the holiday pics and a few million of my fave tunes... oh yeah, and did I mention it's really cool?

I was a bit nervous about meeting Uncle Tad (or should I address him as 'Professor'?) as we hadn't seen each other since I was about ten, but I was reassured the minute I saw him waiting at the arrivals gate at Naples airport. He's not quite as tall as I remember, but the salt-and-pepper hair and beard are just about the same, only a bit more salt than pepper now. He's got Mom's eyes, only more crinkly round the edges, especially when he smiles. With the tan and the fedora, there's a touch of Indiana Jones about him.

I don't remember my aunt; she died when I was two. But Mom says ever since then Uncle Tad just buried himself in his work. Romantic, in a sad kind of way.

He shook hands (very formal) then kissed me on both cheeks (very European). We threw my bags into the back of his incredibly beat-up old pickup truck and got onto the autostrada, which is about as picturesque as the New Jersey Turnpike – until you get away from the airport and pass vineyards and olive groves and, towering over everything, the volcano Vesuvius – enormous and totally awesome. And a bit scary.

Uncle Tad talked non-stop all the way to Pompeii, mainly about his new project. He thinks he's discovered the legendary Villa Deidamia, mentioned by Pliny the Younger (some ancient Roman guy) and one of the lost treasures of antiquity. Deidamia, he told me, was a Greek princess and married to Achilles.

My mind was reeling a bit at all this history, but, not wanting to sound like a total moron, I said, "I thought Achilles was a confirmed bachelor." Uncle Tad laughed a lot at that and said he was glad I knew my Greek mythology. Fact is, I think I heard it on Jeopardy.

Memo: Go online and find out who 'Pliny the Younger' is.

Monday, July 11

The Pensione Excelsior doesn't quite live up to its name, but it's clean and the bathroom is in the room, not down the hallway as I'd feared. It's quite small, and Signora Zingarelli (4 feet tall and spherical) runs the place almost single-handed. She's very nice, although when I asked about room service her answer was vague to say the least.

The hotel breakfast buffet looked like it had been there for about a week, so I went down the street to a little sidewalk café. I was really pleased to discover the waiter understood me when I ordered in Italian – all those afternoons reading 'Corriere della Sera' to Grandpa finally paid off! He used to pay me 50 cents an article, and was a demon for correct pronunciation.

My coffee had just arrived when this incredibly scruffy-looking dog came and sat at my feet and gazed up at me with these enormous brown eyes. He really was pretty cute, jet black all over, except for a white patch on his chest, one dirty white paw and one ear hanging at half-mast. He wagged his tail slowly and looked badly in need of a handout. I was just about to give him a bit of my pastry when disaster struck. The waiter must have tripped over him, because suddenly plates of food were flying around like UFOs, and there was scrambled eggs, ham, cheese and coffee all over everything – including me!

The restaurant owner (Signor Umberto, 300 pounds, one eyebrow) rushed up and started apologizing to me and yelling at the dog and the waiters, all at the same time.

A table of construction workers thought this was hilarious. They laughed and slapped their sides – then they realized it was their breakfast all over the sidewalk, so they joined in the yelling. Then one of them slipped on an omelet and fell on his backside. His buddy laughed, so the guy got up and slugged him. Italians!! Is 'volatile' the right word?

Wait, there's more: Then the other waiter dropped his hose and it writhed around on the ground spraying water over everyone. I just wanted out of there so I could shower and change before I met up with Uncle Tad, but there was even worse to come.

Out of nowhere, this totally mean-looking guy in a black suit and matching eye-patch appeared and grabbed the dog by the scruff of its neck.

"Thees dog," (his English was about as good as my Italian) "he geev you trouble Signorina?"

"No! No!" I didn't want to get the poor dog into even more trouble than he was in. But the scarfaced guy dropkicked the dog into the street, right into the face of a boy driving by on a Vespa.

The Vespa went one way, the boy went the other, and his books and papers flew all over the place. I hurried over to him.

"You all right?"

He picked himself up and hauled his scooter back upright.

"Perché hai passi il cane?" he yelled at me.

"Excuse me?"

"Why you throw your dog at me?"

"I didn't throw anything! This man..." I looked around, but there was no sign of the one-eyed guy. "He was right here, he had a black eye patch and a scar and he kicked..."

The boy tore off his helmet and I noticed he was good looking, kind of, in an Italian sort of way – a mass of black hair sticking up in all the wrong places, and surprisingly deep blue eyes.

"You should keep your dog on a leech."

"That'd be *leash*! And it's not my dog!" I tried to help him collect his papers and stuff from the gutter.

"You mix them up!" he yelled.

I dropped them right back in the gutter. "I'm not doing it on purpose! And anyway, you should watch where you're going! You could've killed that poor creature!"

"So? Is only a dog."

Only a dog! "What a jerk!"

"Jerk? Non capisco."

"That's English for 'jerk', JERK!"

I turned on my heel and went back to the café, where the waiter gave me a towel to get the egg off my face. Signor Umberto offered me dinner on the house tonight and I'll probably take him up on it.

I've got no idea what happened to the dog. The guy with the eye-patch probably strangled it.

CHAPTER 3

NERO'S MEMOIRS

I was hoping to get to know you a bit better before I broke the news about my, shall we say, ancestry, but it's too late now. There's no getting away from it – I'm a dog, and if you've got a problem with that, you might as well stop reading.

When I say I'm a dog, I should explain that I'm not just any dog. I'm one of the Dogs of Pompeii, a proud and ancient race of canines who can trace their lineage back over two thousand human years. You never heard of us? Most people haven't, but if you ever go to Pompeii you'll notice quite a number of dogs in the ruins of the ancient city.

There have always been dogs in Pompeii, ever since wolves came out of the mountains and conned humans into feeding them. Old Augustus (he's the Leader of the Pack) always says, "That's all Pompeii is these days: dogs and ruins, ruins and dogs." He's quite a philosopher, that Augustus.

If you don't know about the destruction of Pompeii, look it up someplace else. I'm not running a history class here. But I will tell you about the part the dogs played on that momentous day. The story's been handed down from dog to dog for two thousand years (human years that is), and Augustus swears it's true. To get the full dramatic value you really need to hear him tell it – he tears himself to shreds and has to lie down in the shade for hours afterwards. But in his absence, I'll do the best I can.

August, 79 AD.

Way back then, Pompeii was a nice little seaside getaway for rich Romans, with beautiful buildings and parks, a sports arena, two theatres, temples, markets, bath houses – all in the shadow of the volcano.

But something was seriously wrong.

For weeks before the fatal day, there were warning signs. The ground shook, wells and springs dried up and no birds sang. But the humans just went about their business – only the dogs took heed. With their superior senses, they could feel the tremors long before the humans. A few dogs tried to make their owners aware of the danger, but without success.

The tremors increased. The Leader of the Pack called an emergency meeting. He announced that if the humans ignored the portents, the dogs would not. So he and a handful of dogs left the city through Porta di Sarno and headed out into unknown country.

They walked for a day and a night without rest into the hot summer breeze, keeping Vesuvius downwind. On the second day the wind died down and all was quiet. Suddenly, the eerie silence was shattered by a tremendous explosion.

A gigantic column of smoke erupted from the top of Mount Vesuvius, rising twenty miles into the sky, before falling back to earth, scalding the countryside with burning ash and rock.

CHAPTER 3

The eruption continued for two whole days and nights. The dogs ran farther, higher, into the hills, often unable to breathe or to see in the smoke-filled air. Some fell with exhaustion and were left behind. Eventually, the survivors found shelter and slept.

On the third morning, they woke to a scene of total devastation. Pompeii had vanished, buried beneath a blanket of smoldering ash that stretched as far as the eye could see. Owners, families, friends – all were gone.

The Leader addressed the survivors. "We are all powerless against the forces of nature, but dogs are wiser than men. The Dogs of Pompeii will remember this day forever!" And that's a long time for a dog. "We will watch over Pompeii and if her hour of need comes again, we dogs will not fail in our duty a second time."

And so the pact was made. The dogs would hand down the story from generation to generation, dog to dog. They sealed the pact with a solemn vow – CAVE CANEM, which, as you probably know is Latin for BEWARE OF THE DOG. And whoever would bring harm to Pompeii would do well to heed that warning.

For centuries the city slept deep beneath the caked ash and Pompeii was forgotten – but not by the dogs.

Then one day men returned to Pompeii and began to uncover the buried city. And the dogs returned with them.

To this day the most sacred spot for us in all the city is the pavement mosaic at the entrance to the House of the Tragic Poet. It shows a chained guard dog with the words 'Cave Canem' inscribed underneath. Every time we pass it, we think of that long-ago dog who died at his post and the vow our ancestors made.

CHAPTER 4

NERO'S MEMOIRS

Where was I? Oh, yeah – flying through the air and landing smack in the face of the kid on the Vespa. But don't panic. I fell on my feet – all four of them.

Caroline and the kid on the scooter started yelling at each other. In fact, everyone in the cafe was yelling at everyone else. I thought it was time for me to take a powder, so I got as low to the ground as I could and crept away.

Most mornings, after breakfast, I meet up with my buddy Rufus. Don't let the terrible jokes or the goofy expression fool you: he's a true friend and loyal. Too bad about his ears, though. They look as if he borrowed them from a bigger dog.

"Whassup, cat got your tongue?" Rufus grinned that silly grin of his with his tongue hanging out of his mouth as if this was the wittiest thing a dog had ever said.

I was still a bit shaken up by the Umberto incident. I'd been kicked out of better joints than that – what was bugging me was that I'd been humiliated in front of Caroline. But I didn't want to tell Rufus any of that. He's a good guy, but not exactly brimming with sensitivity, so I said, "Just hungry."

"Something to eat, you'll be fine." Rufus looked around as though a pepperoni pizza was going to appear out of thin air. "Lessee" he said thoughtfully. "No tourists for at least another hour. Hows about we go over to the new dig site and see what we can get outta the geeks?" 'Geek' is Rufus's name for an archaeologist. I was considering the proposal when Augustus approached.

I suppose you'd call Augustus the 'alpha dog'. To us, he's the Leader of the Pack, directly descended (he says) from the dog who led the pack out of ancient Pompeii. This may well be true; he's big and shaggy and his coat has so many different colors, he looks like he's descended from every dog who ever lived. He's getting on a bit, but he still commands a lot of respect.

"Nero, my boy!" He glanced from us to the mosaic of the chained dog. "Glad to see you're brushing up on your history. We Dogs of Pompeii should always remember our proud heritage!" He gave Rufus a cursory nod and Rufus stopped panting long enough to greet him.

"Hey Gus, how's it hangin'?"

Rufus is the only dog in Pompeii who can get away with calling Augustus 'Gus', but that doesn't mean Augustus approves; he raised his nose a little higher and snorted. But Rufus never knows when to quit.

"C'mon Gus, why the long face?" Then he rolled on the ground yelping with laughter. "*Why the long face!*"

Augustus ignored him and turned to me. "You seem troubled Nero my boy."

"Bit of a run-in at Umberto's this morning."

Augustus shrugged his big old shoulders raising a cloud of dust. "Well, if you insist on frequenting such establishments...." Augustus has never approved of my working Umberto's – thinks it's beneath me. He should talk! Like, bumming stale sandwiches from old ladies in the Stabian Baths is a higher calling?

"And as for Signor Umberto, you know the old saying: lie down with dogs, you get up with fleas."

Rufus and I exchanged a mystified glance.

"A figure of speech," Augustus said, scratching himself. "Always remember Nero, the watchword of a Dog of Pompeii is 'dignity'." He gave Rufus a disdainful glance as he said this.

Rufus stretched. "Well, I dunno about you guys, but I'm starving. Whaddaya say we go over to the new dig site and hit up the geeks? They're always good for a slice of salami."

Augustus shuddered and raised another cloud of dust. "Forgive me if I decline. Students of archaeology are not known for the refinement of their palates. One finds a better class of tourist at the Stabian Baths."

He turned away. Our audience with the Leader was over, so Rufus and I set out for the dig.

"However..." Augustus was right behind us. "I'm always interested in the welfare of my pack, so perhaps I'll accompany you." Rufus snickered. Augustus gave him a stern look. "But don't expect me to demean myself by *begging*."

We got to the dig just in time for morning break. I saw what Augustus meant about archaeologists and their eating habits. Their morning snack was nothing more than bologna sandwiches and a few wrinkled apples – and they weren't about to share with anyone.

Professor Garibaldi was droning on and on as usual about how this was the site of the lost Villa Something-Or-Other mentioned in the letters of Pliny the Younger, whoever he is. The professor's always talking about this Pliny guy and how he wishes he'd written more letters. Maybe he would if the professor wrote back once in a while. To tell the truth I don't understand archaeology. They never seem to find anything useful and even if they do find a bone, there's never any meat on it.

Suddenly there was a welcome interruption.

"Sorry I'm late."

It was Caroline!

CHAPTER 5

CAROLINE'S JOURNAL

Monday, July 11

continued

It took me a while to get cleaned up. My shorts and shirt were soaked with coffee and egg. So I changed my shorts and put on a bikini top. They seemed appropriate for the weather, at any rate. I slathered myself with sunblock, put on my biggest straw hat, dark sunglasses and shoved a few essentials into a beach bag.

The day was heating up and tourists were beginning to arrive, busload after busload. At Porta Marina, I showed my special pass to the guide. Porta Marina was the main entrance to the city in ancient times and led directly up from the seaport.

The guide explained that Uncle Tad's dig was at the other end of the city, just outside the city wall. I walked the length of Via dell'Abbondanza – Pompeii's main street. It's paved with large flat stones and at the end of every block, there are stepping stones for the pedestrians, with grooves between for chariot wheels.

I passed painted walls, columns that once supported great temples and rows of what must have been shops. A large grassy field bordered by arches flanked a sports arena that would put Giant's Stadium in the shade. I was staggered by the size of the city. It must've been quite a place two thousand years ago!

I was also surprised by how many dogs there are here, dusty looking mutts, but they all look friendly. I saw a guide calling one of them by name and giving it some of his breakfast.

Porta di Sarno, the gateway at the far end of this long avenue, was bricked up long ago. So a guide led me through a little gate in the wall and I got my first glimpse of Villa Deidamia.

I have to admit I was a bit disappointed – I guess I've seen too many Roman epics. A big rocky area of red, dusty earth was criss-crossed by shallow trenches with the tops of brick walls visible here and there. The plan of the villa was marked out with strips of yellow tape. It looked a bit like a crime scene in a TV cop show.

Uncle Tad was addressing a group standing by a large tent. Some were adults, some were young students who, like me, were there to work on the dig during their summer break. All of them were wearing jeans or overalls, scruffy work shirts and hard hats. I did a quick assessment of what I had on – but it was too late to go back and change.

Everyone seemed riveted by what Uncle Tad was saying.

"The mystery we have to solve is, why was such a grand house built outside the city walls? Was the owner an outcast? If so, he was a very rich outcast, judging by the size of the villa."

"Sorry I'm late" I said.

Uncle Tad glanced my way. "Sorry Signorina, tourists are not permitted at this site." He turned back to the group. "In Greek mythology, Deidamia was..."

"It's *me* uncle Tad. Your niece, Caroline."

CHAPTER 5

He took a closer look. So did most of the students. A few of them sniggered. "*Caroline?*" Uncle Tad looked at me as if I'd come for Halloween on the wrong day. "Why on earth are you dressed like that?"

Now some of the students laughed outright. I blushed right through my sunblock.

"I had to change, there was egg all over my..."

"Everybody!" Uncle Tad turned to the group. "This is my niece Caroline from New Jersey. She is going to –" He broke off as he inspected me from head to toe, "– assist us with the excavation."

A woman in a khaki shirt and dusty blue jeans separated herself from the group. "Welcome to Pompeii Caroline dear!" she said in some sort of British accent.

"My associate" Uncle Tad said. "Doctor Innes-McGregor."

"Fiona" she said with a warm smile and I felt better about looking like a dork. "University of Edinburgh. I specialize in First and Second Century Ceramics, and..." with a sidelong glance at Uncle Tad. "... marriage customs in the ancient world."

I have to say she seems an unlikely expert on marriage, ancient or modern and, in spite of her adoring glances at Uncle Tad, I don't think he has a clue she's got anything on her mind except old ruins. For someone who's younger than my mom, Fiona is (let's face it) not exactly glamorous. Nothing that couldn't be fixed! But she's one of those people who's so obsessed with her work that little things like lipstick are way down on her list. If she'd just take off those glasses, use a little foundation, and either keep her hair up or let it down altogether – every time there's a breeze, she has to pick strands of it out of her mouth. I made a mental note to get her a copy of 'Bobbi Brown's Makeup Tips' and perhaps send it to her anonymously.

She introduced me to the students who, in spite of the sniggers, seemed nice enough. There are about twenty of them. One of them offered me a hardhat and a work shirt to keep the sun off my shoulders. Then the archaeologists introduced themselves. What a bunch of oddballs! Nobody said, "Hi, I'm Susanna," or anything like that. They all said stuff like, "Susanna Chang, BA, BSc Shanghai University, specializing in Archaeobotany – or "Pietro Bruni, MA, PhD, University of Milan, Cognitive Anthropology", and scariest of all, "Helmut Heimgarten, MPhil, Universitat Leipzig, Dietary Reconstruction from Latrine Deposits." Yuk.

I felt I should come up with something like, "Caroline Donohue, Clairmont High, majoring in texting, mall trawling and iPod", but I figured no one would get the joke.

Fiona took my arm and said she'd walk me round the site. Uncle Tad waved us off absent-mindedly and went on with his lecture.

We stumbled over rocks and kicked up a lot of dust, stepping over yellow tape as Fiona described what they believe is below us, buried under twenty feet of solid volcanic ash. She's really passionate about it all. She pointed out where different rooms might be, and what might be in them and it all started to come to life for me. The scale of the project is daunting. They figure it'll be five years before the entire villa is unearthed. As she talked and guided me round, always making sure she explained things so a newbie like me could understand, I felt I'd made my first friend in Pompeii. We returned to Uncle Tad who was still in full oration mode.

"If my research is correct, somewhere below us is the bronze statue of Deidamia – the statue that Pliny said was the most beautiful in all the world. I know some historians consider it to be a myth, but finding the statue will be our priority."

The group applauded and I joined in. Then I heard a voice I recognized.

"Mi scusa professore."

It was Mr Congeniality himself – the jerk who fell off the Vespa!

"Gianni! About time!" Uncle said. "Our sponsor will be here at any minute and we must show him our progress report..." The jerk handed over a sheaf of dirty, crumpled papers and Uncle Tad looked as if the sky had fallen on him. "What is this? *Mud*?"

"A slight accident Professore. A girl threw a dog at me and..."

"I did *not* throw the dog!" I yelled. The jerk whirled round and looked at me like it was a bank holdup.

"*Quest'è la ragazza!*"

"The ragazza is my nipote" Uncle Tad said irritably. "I mean, the *girl* is my *niece*! English *please!*" He shuffled through the crumpled papers. "I can't give these to our sponsor! This is a privately funded project! We depend on his money!"

The jerk shuffled his feet. "There was no time to run off new copies." The poor guy looked so miserable, I had to say something. It all came out in a stupid rush.

"It's my fault, well sort of, see I was having breakfast and there was this little black dog and this really mean-looking guy in a black suit with this eye patch and he kicked the dog smack into Gianni and the dog knocked him clear off his scooter and I thought what a creep and Gianni's like why did you throw your dog at me and hey I didn't throw the dog and all the papers got kinda you know and they're only a bit crumpled so maybe I could like iron them or something?"

Everyone looked at me as if I'd lost it. Uncle Tad hadn't taken his eyes off the muddied papers, but when he realized I'd stopped talking he looked up and gave us a vague wave of his hand.

"I'm glad you two have already met. You'll be working together."

CHAPTER 6

CAROLINE'S JOURNAL

Monday, July 11

continued

Gianni and I spoke simultaneously.

"Work with *her*?"

"Work with *him*?"

"Find something for her to do!" Uncle Tad said impatiently.

Before either of us could object further, a big black Mercedes roared onto the site, and skidded to a halt scattering the students. When the dust cleared, who should get out but Scarface!

"That's him! That's the guy who kicked the dog!" But no one paid any attention to me.

Scarface was shouting orders into a headset as he opened the rear door to let out three people – two sinister looking men in black suits and dark glasses, and a short fat guy in a crumpled gray suit clutching a briefcase as if his life depended on it. Then there was a sound like thunder. We all looked up as a sleek, silver helicopter came out of the sky. On its side were the words: MACCHIATO TUTTOMONDO. We shielded our faces against the dust as it landed smack in the middle of the dig site scattering yellow tape in all directions.

Fiona gasped as she watched her work being shredded, and clutched at Uncle Tad who looked grim, but patted her hand reassuringly. If *they* seemed shocked, Gianni looked ready to kill.

The helicopter door opened and out stepped this stocky man with hair too black to be natural. He wore a cream linen suit and puffed on a huge cigar and looked as if he owned the world, or at least half of it. His sunglasses were only slightly darker than his tan.

"Mister Money?" I asked Gianni.

"Signor Macchiato" Gianni said between clenched teeth.

A tall, glamorous blonde in an incredibly short white dress followed him down the steps. I guess she wasn't afraid of heights, because she was wearing the highest heels I've ever seen. She wore lots, and I mean *lots* of gold jewelry – bracelets, chains, necklaces, brooches. I wondered how she managed to stay vertical. Gianni wondered too, but for a different reason. His eyes were fixed on her neckline.

"Mamma mia" he said. "She is... how you say in English?"

"Trophy wife" I said.

Scarface passed us as he walked to meet them. I was about to give him a piece of my mind for kicking defenseless dogs, when he turned and gave me a look that could've frozen water. I kept my mouth shut. The way he shadowed Signor Macchiato, I figured he was some kind of bodyguard. I made a mental note to steer clear of him. Uncle Tad stepped over the tangle of yellow tape to greet the Macchiatos.

"Professor Garibaldi!" Signor Macchiato smiled, exposing a lot of expensive dental work. "Wonderful to see you again!" They shook hands. "My wife, Sofronia." Signora Macchiato extended a limp hand. Uncle Tad did the European thing and kissed it.

"Signor, Signora – welcome to Villa Deidamia."

Signor Macchiato looked around. "And now to the Villa. Which way do we go?"

There was an awkward pause. Finally Uncle Tad said, "You're there already."

Signor Macchiato's smile slipped a bit. "Scusi?"

"You're standing on it. Or rather, twenty feet above it."

The smile slipped right off Macchiato's face. "You mean, this is it?"

I knew exactly what was happening. Uncle Tad could visualize the Villa in all its pre-eruption splendor, but all Signor Macchiato could see was a pile of dirt!

They started talking fast in Italian, too fast for me to follow, but I could tell Macchiato was asking a lot of difficult questions. After a while Uncle Tad took him off by himself to show him the rest of the site.

"I go to the Professor" Gianni said. "He needs..." he searched for the English, "...support for his morals."

"That'd be moral support" I offered, but Gianni was gone. I searched for some shade and there, under a tree, sat the little black dog from Umberto's cafe. On either side of him were two of the scruffiest dogs I've ever seen – a big, old, multi-colored dog, and one with long ears and a goofy grin. I knelt and stroked the black dog's head.

"Hey little fella. Glad to see you're okay." He gazed up at me with those big brown eyes and his tail wagged slowly.

"Are these your buddies?" I patted the big, shaggy dog who raised his head high and looked very serious. Then I turned to the one with the long ears and he broke into a silly grin with his tongue lolling out of the side of his mouth. I couldn't help laughing.

"So!"

The voice made me spin round. Sofronia Macchiato was standing over me. She had a cell phone clamped to her ear – gold, naturally. I scrambled to my feet. She did a quick appraisal of what I was wearing and hated every stitch of it. With her bracelets flashing gold in the sun, she snapped the phone shut and beckoned me to approach. I smiled my most winning smile. She just looked at me as if I had spinach stuck between my teeth.

"You are archaeologist?" she asked. Again my mouth got away from me.

"No, no, I'm Professor Garibaldi's niece I'm just here for the summer he's my uncle on my mother's side the Italian side not the Irish side and I haven't seen him since..." She couldn't care less. She waved a bangled hand around. It jangled a lot.

"This place – it is, how you say – a dump."

I couldn't deny it, so I just shrugged.

She jangled her hand around again. "This so-called Villa, I don't see any..." I tried to help out.

"Walls? ...Floors? ...Ceilings?"

"Artifacts."

"What kind of artifacts?"

"There is no statues, no pretty ancient pots, no – *jewelry*!"

So *that's* what she was getting at! She couldn't care less about archaeology; she was here to shop!

"It's a little soon for that kind of thing" I said trying to sound professional, "but as work progresses I'm sure they'll unearth all sorts of important –"

"*When?*"

It came out like a pistol shot. I felt like a department store clerk explaining that the Spring Sale hadn't started yet.

"Oh, any day now," I said feebly.

"*Five years?*" Signor Macchiato and Uncle Tad were heading towards us and Macchiato's face was like thunder. "The Villa won't be unearthed for *five years*?"

"Not unusual for a project of this size" Uncle said, but Macchiato wasn't listening; he went into a huddle with his entourage. Sofronia used the time to add about ten more coats of lip-gloss.

Finally Macchiato turned to Uncle Tad and said, "Professor, when I signed a contract with you, I was expecting a quicker return on my investment. I'm a lover of antiquity, but I'm also a businessman. I intend to make the Villa a paying proposition."

He snapped his fingers and the little round man in the gray suit shuffled forwards.

"Buon giorno everybody" he said with a jovial smile. "I'm Signor Macchiato's lawyer, Ernesto Spalanzini..."

"No one cares who you are!" Macchiato snapped. He grabbed a wad of colorful brochures from the lawyer and passed them out. "I intend to make the Villa a paying proposition."

As everyone leafed through the brochures, there were gasps of sheer horror.

    Conceived in the lavish spirit
    of our roman ancestors
    THE MACCHIATO
    VILLA DEIDAMIA HOTEL
    &
    ENTERTAINMENT COMPLEX
    a 700-room hotel built directly above
    the site of the fully restored
    VILLA DEIDAMIA

Worse was to come –

    THE MACCHIATO COLOSSEUM
    Three times the size of the original
    and fully air-conditioned!
    presenting
    bloodless gladiatorial combats
    world-class animal acts
    ear-splitting rock concerts

And yet worse –

    The EMPEROR ROOM
    BAR & GRILL
    featuring an authentic 12 course

ROMAN BANQUET

(*non-alcoholic beverages gratis*)

followed by

"POMPEII – THE MUSICAL"

Passion! Greed! Lust! Revenge!

100 singers and dancers 100

ON STAGE NIGHTLY – VESUVIUS ERUPTS!

(*use of cameras and recording devices strictly forbidden*)

In short, Signor Macchiato's plan was to turn Villa Deidamia into a sort of Ancient Roman theme park and make a mockery of my uncle's work!

Uncle Tad was the first to find his voice. He was making a huge effort to stay calm, but I could tell he was beside himself with fury. His voice quivered with emotion.

"Surely, Signor, the Superintendent of Ancient Sites would never allow such a travesty!"

"On the contrary" Macchiato smiled. "*My* money is funding this project. The Superintendent has no say in the matter." He snapped his fingers and Spalanzini the lawyer read nervously from an official-looking document.

"Whereas the Villa Deidamia site is outside the walls of Pompeii, it does not fall under the laws governing excavations within the city. The Superintendent of Ancient Sites will grant Professor Garibaldi until the stroke of noon on Friday, July 22, to find some genuine historical artifact at this site. If nothing of value is found by that date, work on the Macchiato Hotel and Entertainment Complex will commence as planned."

"The 22nd!" Gianni gasped. "That's less than two weeks!"

Macchiato ignored him and snapped his fingers at his wife. "Come, Sofronia. We're expected on Capri for cocktails." He strode to the waiting helicopter, with Sofronia bringing up the rear, teetering across the rubble on Those Shoes. We all stood there speechless. And just when we thought the situation couldn't possibly get any worse, it did.

The little black dog from Umberto's was scrabbling about in the dirt. To be fair to the poor dog, I think he was actually trying to get out of Sofronia's way. Anyway he didn't succeed. One of those spike heels must have caught his tail, because he gave an almighty yelp and shot into the air. Sofronia teetered backwards and fell into a trench. The deepest one. Her scream could've been heard in Naples. Florida.

We all hurried to the edge. Sofronia was flat on her back, her hair a muddy mess. One shoe no longer had a spike heel and the little white dress would never be the same again. Macchiato yelled "Somebody do something!"

Uncle Tad tore off his hardhat and reached down. Several other students did likewise, but Sofronia knew whose help she wanted. She allowed Uncle Tad to haul her out and lay limp in his arms looking as decorative as she could and fluttering her eyelashes at him. Fiona moved in on the scene like an express train.

"Anything broken?" she asked. "Apart from your hair?"

Sofronia's hand went to her hair and when it came away thick with mud, she screamed again. "That mangy black dog! It's all his fault!"

The little dog tried to back away, but Scarface swooped down and grabbed him up by the scruff of the neck. He turned to Macchiato with a leer.

"Whaddya say boss, you want I throttle him now?"

CHAPTER 7

NERO'S MEMOIRS

I don't know why these stupid things always happen to me. Look at Rufus: he's nowhere near as smart as I am, but he sails through life with hardly a scratch.

I was just standing there – okay, I was digging in the dirt – but I was minding my own business and, contrary to popular opinion, I did not trip up Signora Macchiato. *She* trod on *my* tail – and I still feel it in damp weather. Next thing I know, this thug with the eye-patch grabs me by the scruff of the neck and starts carrying on like he wants to kill me!

Then Signora Macchiato joined in – or should I say screamed in. "What are all these dogs doing here anyway? Dirty filthy things! Get rid of them!"

And Signor Macchiato added his five cents worth at the top of his voice. "*All these dogs must go!*"

The one-eyed thug tightened his grip on my neck. I couldn't look at Caroline I was so embarrassed. I was also choking. But it was Caroline who saved the situation. She walked right up to the goon, cool as you like, looked him straight in his only visible eye, and said, "Drop the dog."

It was a standoff.

The thug stared at her coldly for a long time, then looked over to Signor Macchiato, who nodded. "Put the dog down, Monocolo."

"Scusi, Signorina, I didn't know this mongrel was your *pet*." He spat the word out as if it tasted bad, and tossed me to the ground like a stale sandwich.

I got out of there as fast I as could, with Rufus and Augustus right behind me. I don't think Augustus had moved that fast in years. We didn't stop running until we got to the Grand Palaestra – that's a big grassy square surrounded by arches and shady trees. It was an open air gym in ancient times, but now us dogs hang there.

We threw ourselves down in the shade. Rufus and I were pretty winded, but poor old Augustus was nearly a goner. Needless to say, he was furious with me.

"What in the name of the gods were you *doing* Nero?" I couldn't look him in the eye. "I... was looking for my tennis ball."

"*A tennis ball*?"

I should explain, tennis is this weird human game where they hit the ball instead of fetching it. Go figure. I used to play fetch with old Giuseppe the guide. Then, when they started digging up the place, we couldn't play there any more. But some things stick in your memory, and that tennis ball was one of them.

"A tennis ball" Augustus gasped, and flopped onto his side.

"It's got sentimental value" I said apologetically.

Rufus was horrified. "Not the good one, with all the slobber on it?"

We lay silent for a while – except for the panting. Then Rufus sat up and looked thoughtful, which is a bit of a stretch for him.

CHAPTER 7

"So! This Signor Macaroni guy wants to build a big hotel. Hotel – tourists! Tourists – food!"

"Aren't you forgetting something?" Augustus asked wearily.

Rufus went over the equation in his head – "Hotel, tourists, food... nope."

"All these dogs must go."

Rufus put his head on one side. "What does that mean?"

"It means" Augustus said with a sigh, "that dogs won't be welcome at that hotel."

Rufus's jaw dropped open. You're kidding!"

"Thanks to Nero."

Now I *really* felt good. I was just about to apologize all over again when Rufus's pretty little cousin Olivia came bounding up to us. She's part greyhound on her father's side, so she can really move.

"Rufus, come quickly! It's Drusilla!"

Rufus leapt up. "You mean...?

"Yes! The pups have arrived!"

Rufus turned in a circle and did a little jump. "Oh boy! *Oh boy*! I'm a *father*!" He raced off after Olivia. Augustus struggled wearily to his feet.

"More mouths to feed."

I followed slowly. I had a lot on my mind and, let's face it, happy as I was for Rufus, I'm not much of a family man.

Drusilla and the puppies were in a shady nook inside a partially excavated house. The pups were already feeding, tucked in close to Drusilla's body. Drusilla was always a beauty (in the way part-Spaniels usually are), but today she was positively radiant. Rufus was surrounded by well-wishers and looked as if he'd burst with pride.

A crowd of dogs had gathered. A new litter is a real event in Pompeii – it doesn't do to overpopulate. I hung about at the edge of the group. Rufus nosed his way through the dogs looking for me.

"Whattaya say Nero?"

"Congratulations buddy. What are you going to call them?"

"Gee, I dunno!" He turned to Drusilla, "what do you think we should call them honey?"

Drusilla looked up and said "No Rufus, you should name them."

Rufus cocked his head on one side. "Lessee – four boys and a girl. How about Primus, Secundus, Tertius, Quartus and Quinta."

"Very original" Drusilla said lovingly.

Suddenly I was tongue-tied. All I could think of to say was, "At least these kids will know who their dad is," which hardly seemed appropriate. Also, there was something in my eye – dust from the street, I expect. Olivia looked concerned.

"Are you all right Nero?"

I just nodded and walked away.

I went back to the Grand Palaestra and sat on the grass watching the groups of tourists go by. A few of them took my picture and held out bits of leftover food, but the events of the day had taken away my appetite. Signor Macchiato's words rang in my ears – "*All these dogs must go!*"

What kind of life could the new pups expect? Our whole world seemed to be on the brink of change – just how dramatic that change would be I couldn't begin to imagine.

CHAPTER 8

CAROLINE'S JOURNAL

Monday 11th July

continued

My first day in Pompeii has been pretty eventful.

Tonight Uncle Tad, Fiona, Gianni and I had dinner at Umberto's. The little black dog wandered cautiously into the restaurant and I beckoned to him. He slipped under the table and sat at my feet. Tony, the waiter, winked at me and said "His name is Nero, Signorina. But don't let Signor Umberto see him." Now and then, I slipped him a piece of ham from our antipasto platter and he took it from me gently.

Signor Umberto could see that Uncle Tad was upset about something and took it upon himself to wait on us personally.

"Some wine, Signor Professore?" he asked solicitously.

My uncle sighed. "I suppose so. You choose for us, Umberto."

"And for the Signorina?" he beamed at me.

"Bring her a Chinotto." Gianni said with an annoying smirk. Boy he's obnoxious. Chinotto is a kind of Italian cola – sticky dark brown stuff, composed (at a rough guess) of melted-down licorice sticks and cough medicine – and no self-respecting person over the age of ten would be caught dead drinking it.

The wine arrived, but it did little to lighten Uncle Tad's mood. He gazed gloomily at the gaudy brochure outlining Signor Macchiato's plans for his resort.

"All my life, I've believed that by studying the past we can make a better future for the world. Macchiato seems only concerned with making a better future for himself." His gloom turned to anger and he crumpled the brochure and thrust it into a pocket.

"There is no better way of judging the future than by the past," Gianni said, and added pompously, "Edward Gibbon, 1737 to 1794."

Smartass, I thought. There was a long silence. I tried to think of something encouraging to say.

"Hey, c'mon Uncle Tad. Don't let this Macchiato guy get you down. So what if he builds his stupid hotel? Maybe you can dig up some other old ruin."

Fiona and Gianni looked as if I'd suggested setting fire to an orphanage.

"Archaeology is not just about digging up some old ruin" Uncle Tad explained patiently. "It's not about something old and dead, it's about *life*! What do you see when you walk in the streets of Pompeii?"

I thought really hard. "Old houses? Broken columns? Peeling paintings?"

"What about *the people*?"

"You mean the tourists?"

"No, the people who lived here two thousand years ago! Those 'old houses' can tell us how they lived – the paintings show us what made them happy or sad, what they thought about, what their dreams were!"

I felt about five years old and considered crawling under the table with the dog. Fiona put an arm around my shoulder.

"Pompeii is *the* most important historic site in the whole world, but it's in danger of being destroyed all over again – by lack of funding, by carelessness..."

"*By people like Macchiato!*" Uncle Tad thundered. "He would raze Pompeii to the ground if he thought he could make a few more millions!" He thumped the table with his fist and Nero jumped with fright.

"Shh, Taddeo" Fiona said, "you're scaring the waiters."

Not to mention the dogs.

Uncle Tad put his head in his hands. "If only we could find the statue of Deidamia! She *must* be there! My research *cannot* be wrong!

No one said much as they walked me back to my hotel. I tried to get a word or two out of Gianni. "So, this Deidamia – was there something special about her?"

"She was a princess" Gianni said, as if everyone in the world knew it but me. "In Greek mythology, she was in love with Achilles. Have you ever heard of him?" he asked in a supercilious kind of way.

"Sure I have! I saw the movie 'Troy' ten times."

He rolled his eyes.

"It was a kid thing!" I said a little too defensively. "My best friend Didi Carr had a crush on Brad Pitt! Have *you* ever heard of *him*?"

"Americans! Do you understand anything about history?"

This brought out the Irish in me. "I suppose you Italians are the Keepers Of The Holy Grail Of The Olden Days or something!"

"'Those who fail to learn from history are doomed to repeat it' – George Santayana, 1863 to 1952."

I couldn't think of a smart comeback, so I just said "Dweeb."

"What does it mean, this 'dweeb'?"

"It's a nice way of saying 'know-it-all'."

He smiled modestly. "*Grazie tante*. But I don't know it *all*! Not yet, anyway."

He thought it was a compliment! I tried not to crack up. "You're welcome." I caught up with my uncle and Fiona. "Uncle Tad, I want to help! I *really* want to help."

Uncle Tad looked a bit stuck for something to say. I figured he didn't think I was capable of working with real live archaeologists, so I rambled on. "I mean digging's digging, right? I'm cool with a pick and shovel." Gianni rolled his eyes again. "Bucket and spade?"

Fiona brushed a few strands of hair off her face. "Try eggcup and spoon" she said gently.

"You're kidding me."

"Excavation is very delicate work" Gianni said as if he knew all about it.

"And we have less than two weeks" the Professor said glumly.

"There must be *something* I can do!"

Fiona smiled warmly. "We'll find something."

She nudged Uncle Tad who nodded and murmured "We have an early start tomorrow." He held my shoulders gently, kissed me on both cheeks and smiled. "So like your mother.

Buona notte cara." And he and Fiona walked away down the dark street.

Gianni just said "You should get your – what do Americans call it? Beauty sleep." And he walked away without even saying good night. What a royal pain in the ass.

I felt something cold and wet touch my ankle and looked down to see Nero gazing up at me. I sat on the doorstep of the hotel and stroked his head.

"Well, at least I've got one buddy in Pompeii."

CHAPTER 9

NERO'S MEMOIRS

The good news was meeting Caroline – this was the beginning of a beautiful friendship – as my hero Bogie might have put it

The bad news was that life was going to the dogs – as someone who didn't know much about dogs once said.

In the next few days, the whole feeling of the city changed. Everywhere we dogs went, we were moved on. One day old Giuseppe the guide lost his temper and kicked Augustus out of the Stabian Baths. Augustus wasn't bothering anybody, just taking a nap in the shade, like he does every afternoon.

Giuseppe yelled, "This is a museum site, not a dog's home!" Nothing like that had ever happened before. We thought of Giuseppe as our friend, especially Augustus, because they'd grown old together.

I went out to take a look at the Villa Deidamia dig. The geeks were swarming over it, working ten times harder than they had before. The Professor insisted that Caroline work with Gianni. Not a good idea. She was being extra careful, but she accidentally knocked a bucket of earth over.

"Idiot!" Gianni yelled. "There might be something valuable in that bucket!"

"Not if you put your stupid head in it" Caroline yelled back.

I was at a loose end, and bored, and whenever I felt that way, my mind wandered back to my old tennis ball. It *had* to be here somewhere! I stayed well away from Caroline and Gianni and had a little dig of my own. My paw struck something solid – I dug harder. But it wasn't my ball, it was a metal hand. It looked to be waving – hello or goodbye, it's hard to tell with humans. Maybe this was something the geeks might find important. I barked to catch the Gianni kid's attention.

He just shouted at me. "Cane stupido! Go away!"

Then Caroline shouted at him. "Don't yell at Nero, he's not hurting anyone!"

The Professor headed our way and looked pretty angry. I didn't want him to think I was doing anything I shouldn't, so I turned my back to the metal hand and, with a few thrusts of my hind paws, covered it up with dirt again.

"You two are getting on my nerves" the Professor said. "You've been bickering all morning! You should take a day off."

Gianni dropped his spade. "Assolutamente *no*!"

"*Assolutamente yes*! Tomorrow, take Caroline to the beach!"

Caroline and Gianni looked at each other as if they'd rather eat dogfood.

"But we've only got one more week!" Caroline said, almost in tears.

"I insist! The Mediterranean air will do you good. It will clear your heads! And *mine*! You'll work all the harder for having a day off!"

CHAPTER 9

Whenever Bogie felt down, he asked this guy called Sam to play the piano. I didn't know anyone called Sam, but I thought if anyone could cheer me up, Rufus was the dog. But he had his own problems.

As the sun went down and the last of the tourists were leaving for the day, I strolled through the deserted streets with him.

"I'm a father Nero. I got responsibilities! If everyone turns against us dogs, where's the food gonna come from? You gotta help me. You know how to work a crowd."

I couldn't deny it. My people skills were the envy of every dog in Pompeii and Rufus had always admired my talent for getting a square meal out of the meanest tourist .

We started out of the city by Porta Marina. He trotted by my side, frowning and murmuring things like "right on" and "awesome" as I taught him a few tricks of the trade.

"Take it slow at first, don't push it. And forget all that stuff about the milk of human kindness, it's a myth. Oh – and if they tell you to sit, sit. They like that for some reason. And if you must wag your tail, do it verrry, verrry slowly – don't let 'em think you're too happy."

Umberto's was busy. I turned to offer a last word of encouragement to my friend and saw a look of sheer terror on his face.

"They're all gonna hate me!"

"A good looking dog like you?"

"He drew himself up to his full height. "You're right. Drusilla always said I was a handsome dog." Then his face fell again. "What if they just ignore me?"

"Simple. Come back later, when they've had a few more drinks."

I gave the tables a professional once-over, looking for a nice easy mark to start him off.

First table: an old married couple who looked as if they hadn't spoken to each other in about twenty-five years. You can never tell with people like that. Sometimes they're happy to see someone worse off than they are; sometimes they're looking for something to kick. It's pretty much a roll of the dice.

As we got closer, the husband's eyes locked with mine and narrowed to slits. A dog-hater from way back.

Next table – a large family with a lot of bratty-looking kids. I decided to give them a miss too.

Another table – a tall skinny guy with a beaky nose, and a short fat guy with a blotchy red face shoveling a pizza into his mouth... and occasionally missing. Uh oh, weirdos.

Then, Bingo – a candle-lit table for two with a young couple gazing into each other's eyes! An encounter with a furry friend would make their evening. I nudged Rufus with my nose. He jumped.

"What! What!"

"Couple in the corner. Go for it."

Rufus gulped. "Now?"

"Now or never. And act natural."

CHAPTER 9

He loped off, looking about as natural as an elephant on a bicycle. I wasn't optimistic. In this line of work, either you've got it or – you're Rufus. But there was nothing more I could do for him. There comes a time when every dog has to stand on his own four paws.

I glanced round to make sure Signor Umberto was nowhere in sight, then turned back to see how Rufus was doing. That's funny, I thought, where is he? He'd gone to the wrong table! The table with the two weirdos!

It all happened so fast.

The sloppy fat one picked Rufus up and ran out into the street with him. The skinny one ran followed looking from side to side to see if anyone had noticed what they were doing.

For a moment, I was so stunned I couldn't move. As they bolted past, Rufus looked at me, eyes wide with surprise.

"What did I do wrong?"

The tall skinny one opened the back door of a little green van and the fat one tossed Rufus inside. In the split second before they slammed the door, I caught sight of several other dogs cowering inside! My pals Julius and Florian and one of Olivia's best friends, little Mira!

These guys were dognappers!

Humphrey Bogart would never let a coupla lowlifes get away with a stunt like this!

I bounded up behind the fat one, stood on my hind legs and sank my teeth into his butt. He yelled, but I hung on.

"Get this one too!" the fat one shouted. I sank my teeth in a bit further. "*Quick!*"

Even with my mouth full, I could snarl, and I did. The skinny guy backed off. The fat one cursed and jumped up and down, but I hung on. Then he swung round and slammed me hard against the side of the van. I dropped to the ground like a stone. But before either of them could grab me, I jumped to my feet and bared every tooth I had. They backed off. By now a couple of passers-by were watching.

"Let's get outta here!" the fat one muttered.

They jumped into the van and drove off with a squeal of tires. I heard an anguished yelp from Rufus as the van rounded the corner at the end of the street.

I followed the van as far as I could, barking like a mad dog, but soon I was left behind, choking on the dust they stirred up.

I ran back to Pompeii as fast as I could and searched for Augustus. He was sleeping in his usual corner of the Palaestra. I barked to wake him up.

"Nero, have you never heard the saying 'let sleeping dogs lie'?"

"We all have to leave the city!"

"Leave?"

"Like *now!* These two ugly humans, a short fat one and a tall skinny one, they dognapped Rufus and they got Julius and Florian and Mira too!"

Augustus sighed and shook his head. "Nero, Nero, Nero, this is what comes of associating with humans. It warps your sense of reality. You've told us so many ridiculous stories about Rick and Elsa and Scarlett and Rhett – whoever they may be. You live in a fantasy world."

I ran round him in circles. "But we have to do something! They're going to take us all away!"

Augustus went into Leader-of-the-Pack mode. "No one's going to take anyone anywhere! We dogs have lived in Pompeii since –"

"Yeah, yeah, I know all that Dogs-of-Pompeii stuff, but this is serious!"

Augustus looked mightily offended. "Perhaps you'll remember your manners after a good night's sleep." He turned over and was snoring almost immediately.

I'll draw a veil over the painful scene of my breaking the news about Rufus's capture to Drusilla. She tried to be brave, but she was grief-stricken and sick with worry. I had no idea why Rufus had been taken, let alone where. I promised to help out with the pups until he was found, it was the least I could do – I know from personal experience what It's like to grow up without a father.

"I'll stay with you tonight and watch the pups," I said. "The pups are the future – maybe the only future we have."

CHAPTER 10

NERO'S MEMOIRS

I didn't get much sleep that night.

Next morning, I headed for Umberto's to get some breakfast for the pups. I turned a corner and – there was the little green van! No one was around, so I approached cautiously and sniffed. I could tell Rufus had been inside, but now the van was empty. I crawled underneath.

Before long, the two weirdos, the short fat one and the tall skinny one, came down the street. The fat one had a Doberman on a leash. I have to admit, I never got on with Dobermans – they all seem to have this chip on their shoulder. The tall skinny one was dragging a big, sad looking dog on a rope – my friend, Marcus!

"Open the door, Luigi!" the fat guy said.

"I got my hands full already!" the skinny one whined.

It was true – Marcus was resisting with all his strength. The fat guy let the Doberman off his leash. "Go get him!" he commanded.

The Doberman ran at poor Marcus, snapping at him until he scrambled whimpering into the back of the van. Luigi, the skinny one, slammed the door shut and wiped his nose with his sleeve.

"Is that it for today, Botti?" he asked hopefully.

"No it's not!" the fat one said. "We been at it since dawn and all we got to show for it is one mangy specimen! And don't call me Botti! The name is Bottiglione – Signor Bottiglione to you."

"Sorry, *Signor*." Luigi faked a respectful bow. "So *Signor*, what now, *Signor*?"

"We keep hunting 'em down till the van's full. Signor Macchiato wants every dog in the place gone. We got six more days to round 'em up and take 'em you-know-where."

Every dog in the place gone?

"Six days?" Luigi sniveled. "But there must be a hundred of 'em, and only two of us!"

"Then you better work a bit faster! Trouble with you is you got no work ethic."

The Doberman caught my scent and growled. Bottiglione got down on the ground and peered under the van.

"Well, what's this?"

His face was so close to mine I could smell the stale wine on his breath. "Open the door, Luigi! Here's another one for you – the dirty little mutt what took a piece outta my rear end!"

Luigi stifled a giggle.

"It ain't funny!" the fat one said as he reached under the van with his stubby arms. I spun round and kicked dirt in his face with my hind legs. He yelled and fell backwards wiping his eyes. Luigi laughed out loud this time.

I saw a flash of white out of the corner of my eye. Olivia! She was heading right for us! The Doberman turned in her direction.

CHAPTER 10

My mind was working double time. I asked myself what Bogart would do in this situation. A diversion! He'd create a diversion! I scrambled out from under the van.

"Olivia!" I barked. "Get out of here now!"

Olivia froze in her tracks.

The Doberman looked from me to her, unsure of who to go for first.

"Go! Take care of Drusilla and the pups!" Olivia took off. The Doberman was about to go after her, but I stood in his way and did my best Bogart impersonation, taunting him out of the side of my mouth.

"Hey you overgrown Dachshund, what are ya waitin' for? Come and get me!"

That did it. He forgot all about Olivia and came straight at me twice as fast as I'd expected. I turned tail and ran. I cleared a low wall in one bound and headed for the amphitheatre. I knew I'd be able to lose him there. Above all, I had to lead him away from the pups.

I charged into the amphitheatre and straight across the arena. I knew it was dangerous to be on open ground, but if I could only get to the arch at the far end, I'd be able to lose him in the maze of passageways beyond. He was so close on my tail, I could feel the heat of his breath. The archway was just up ahead, a black hole in the centre of the sunlit stone. I knew those passages like the back of my paw. He'd never find me there.

I heard the snap of fangs behind me and summoned up one last surge of speed. I was in the tunnel! Any second I'd be out the other end and into safety.

SLAM!

I bounced backwards and landed right at the Doberman's feet. He was as surprised as I was. I'd hit a chain link fence that was blocking the end of the tunnel.

"That wasn't here yesterday!"

"And you won't be here tomorrow" the Doberman sneered, baring some pretty frightening teeth. "Shoulda got outta town when you had the chance Nero."

"How do you know my name?"

"Everyone knows what a slippery customer you are."

I played for time, glancing around to see if there was an escape route. "Gee, guess that makes me Public Enemy Number One." Suddenly, I realized I knew this great lug! "Wait a minute – you're Caligula!"

"What's it to you?" the Doberman growled.

"But why are you working for these losers? You're a Dog of Pompeii – at least your mother was."

"Leave my mother out of this!" he growled. "She's purebred."

I'd hit a nerve, and I knew why. Caligula's mother Agrippina was proud and haughty. Named after an empress, she thought she *was* one. None of the Dogs of Pompeii was good enough for her. Long ago, she went out with Attila, the vicious guard dog from Frascati's Timber and Hardware, another pure-bred Doberman. Together they produced a litter so handsome and sleek they all got adopted. Except Caligula. He was mean-spirited even as a pup, and no one wanted him.

That early rejection just made him meaner. When this Bottiglione guy was recruiting an attack dog, Caligula must have seemed like the perfect candidate. Agrippina always wanted him to be just like his father. She'd got her wish.

The two bozos approached, puffing and panting. Bottiglione held a piece of rope tied in a noose.

"Listen" I said urgently to Caligula, "we could both make a break for it if we..."

"Try it" the Doberman snapped.

Bottiglione thrashed him with the rope. "Get offa him ya dumb canine!"

Caligula retreated with a yelp. Bottiglione turned his attention to me and I growled. He paused and massaged his backside in painful memory of my teeth. He handed the rope to Luigi.

"Get him!"

The skinny guy gulped and moved in on me.

"Here, doggy doggy."

CHAPTER 11

CAROLINE'S JOURNAL

Saturday, 16th July

Almost a week has gone by and I've had no time to bring up the iPad journal let alone actually write anything.

Every morning, I've been at the Villa site at the crack of dawn, doing my best to help dig and sift, putting up with that total pain in the butt Gianni, and hoping against hope that something valuable will show up. So far, nothing. And we only have six more days!

The dogs seem to have got the drift of our anxiety and they stay away from us – or are there fewer dogs than there used to be? I've missed seeing some of the regulars and even Nero doesn't come by much any more. Not surprising after Gianni shouted at him yesterday. Then of course, I shouted at Gianni and Uncle Tad got mad at both of us and ordered us to go to the beach. *Together!*

*

Sunday, July 17

Early this morning, Uncle Tad went to the Archaeological Museum in Naples for research material. I knew all the students and the archaeologists would be hard at work on the dig, and I wanted to see how they were doing before I went anywhere with that creep Gianni, so I headed for the site.

I hurried along Via dell'Abbondanza and was passing the big amphitheatre when I saw these two weirdos, a short fat slob and a tall skinny guy with a big nose. They had Nero with them and he had a rope around his neck! And this vicious looking Doberman was hot on their heels, snarling and slavering. Where were they taking Nero? Maybe this was the explanation for the vanishing dogs!

Nero looked downright tragic and suddenly I knew what the expression 'hangdog' meant. I had to do something.

"Nero, you bad dog!" I shouted. "Where have you been? Come here! Right now!"

Nero did a double take. So did the two weirdos – and even the Doberman looked a bit surprised. The short fat one strutted up to me.

"I am Bottiglione."

"*Signor* Bottiglione" the skinny guy said.

"Shuddup." He stuck his fat nose in right in my face. "This your dog, Signorina?"

I was reeling from the garlic and wine fumes, but I stood my ground and packed as much attitude as I could. "Gotta problem with that?"

He was taken aback by my tone. "Is not a good idea to let your dog run free in Pompeii."

"Why not?"

This threw him. "Why not? Uh, because... because..."

"Because something might happen to him?"

"If he *is* yours, why don't he got a leash?"

"He got a leash!" I said, forgetting all I'd learnt in English class. "But he happens to be so well trained he don't need one – *doesn't* need one! Give me that!" I pulled the rope from the fat guy's hand. "Outta my way!"

Fatso was still in my face. "I warn you Signorina, if I see this dog running loose again, I will be very unhappy."

"And I warn *you*, if I see you mistreating *any* of the dogs, I'll be as *mad as hell*!"

His face turned as red as his nose and he drew himself up to his full height, which was still pretty short. "You threaten Bottiglione?"

"I'm from New Jersey! I threaten anyone I like!"

I turned and marched off with Nero close by my side – and with pretty shaky knees.

There's no doubt those two are rounding up the dogs for Macchiato and – well, I hate to think what their fate might be.

By now it was too late to go to the dig site, so I went straight to Umberto's, where I was to meet Gianni. The rope was still around Nero's neck, so I used it as a leash. Clearly he'd never been on a leash before, because he kept trying to go off in different directions.

Gianni was sitting at a table with three empty espresso cups in front of him.

"So sorry I'm late!" I said as pleasantly as I could manage. He didn't bother to greet me, just looked at Nero suspiciously.

"Why is the dog here?"

I forced myself to speak calmly. "Look – this little fat guy was about to take him away so I lied and said he was mine and if we let him loose now they'll find him again and take him wherever they've taken all the other dogs so if you don't mind I think we'd better take him with us and I know it's a total drag but Signora Zingarelli doesn't allow dogs in the hotel and I don't know what else to do with him."

Gianni looked at me as if I'd escaped from the funny farm, then down at Nero with distaste. "And how are we supposed to take a dog on the scooter?"

I smiled as brightly as I could. "We'll manage."

It took a while to get all three of us onto the thing. I had no choice but to hang onto Gianni, with Nero wedged between us.

I didn't know what to expect of the Amalfi coast, but nothing prepared me for that first heart-stopping vista of cliff, sky and the unbelievably deep blue of the Mediterranean beyond.

The Amalfi Drive – a forty mile series of hairpin bends carved out of the cliff face! A new panorama appeared at every turn, each one more spectacular than the last. Sparkling white houses, hotels and villas seemed to hang in clusters from the cliffs which rose to dizzying heights above us and dropped away perilously to the sea hundreds of feet below.

In the middle of all this beauty, the main emotion (if you're riding on a Vespa) is sheer terror. The road is barely two lanes wide and there's only a low stone wall on the sea side between you and certain destruction on the rocks below. For long stretches it narrows down to a single lane.

There's no sensation quite like hurtling directly at a tour bus that's hurtling directly at you with no intention of stopping! Gianni took it all in his stride, in fact he appeared to speed up whenever he saw a bus approaching. Nor did he linger over any of the spectacular sights along the way. We raced through staggeringly beautiful places without even a glance. It would have been nice to slow down to a hundred miles an hour now and then. It's hard to appreciate all that scenery when your heart's in your mouth.

It didn't help that Gianni spent a lot of the time talking on his cell phone and driving with one hand. I'm sure this is illegal, but I guess no one's told him. I couldn't hear much through my helmet, but I think he was talking to his mother. It sounded like she was annoyed because he'd skipped Sunday lunch with his family.

"Si, si, andando a Ravello, ho detto!' He shouted into the phone. 'Si, *Americana!*'

That'd be me.

Once in a while he lowered the phone and yelled a description of the place we were zipping through.

"Positano! Ancient legend – god of the sea built this town for his great love, Pasitea."

"Very romantic!" I yelled back. "Can we stop and take a...?"

But we didn't.

"Praiano! Interesting Roman ruins here, six hundred B.C. You should see sometime!"

How about now?

"Amalfi! Here, in the fourteenth century, the magnetic compass was invented, by an Italian of course!"

Of course.

At a sign that read RAVELLO, we turned off the coast road, took an even narrower winding road uphill to an unbelievably beautiful square at the top of the mountain. Nero was glad to get his paws onto solid ground – so was I.

I don't think I've ever seen anything so beautiful in my life – and maybe I never will. Gianni filled me in on the history – natch.

"The great Italian writer Boccaccio – 1313 to 1375 – described this coast as the most beautiful in all Italy."

I was so stunned by the view, all I could think to say was "Sure beats the Jersey Shore."

He went on and on as we headed to a cafe on the square. We found a table in the shade and Nero sat at my feet.

"Ravello was founded in the sixth century and was originally..."

This guy had a black belt in boredom.

"...The economic decline of Ravello began in the eleventh century and..."

"Gianni."

"Si?"

"Don't you ever just look at a place and see how beautiful it is?"

"Is beautiful, sure, but you Americans know nothing of our history."

I slammed my coffee cup onto the table and nearly broke it. "Chill!"

"You are cold?"

"I don't want to be here any more than you do! I'd rather be back in Pompeii helping my uncle. Maybe I don't know a thing about old ruins but I do know how much this project means to him. So can we just – be friends? Just for this afternoon?"

Gianni lowered his head for a moment in what could have been shame, then he looked up and said quietly "I also care about the Professor." And he smiled. I mean he *really* smiled. And it altered his entire face! Those deep blue eyes seemed to have a little of the Mediterranean in them.

I smiled back and we relaxed. In fact, if it hadn't been for what happened next, the day would have been pretty near perfect.

It all started with Nero (as usual) being somewhere he shouldn't.

CHAPTER 12

NERO'S MEMOIRS

What a way to travel! In fact I'd go so far as to say It's the *only* way to travel! Caroline kept saying things like, "Wow! Look at the view, look at the view!"

The view?

Check out the *smells*! Air, earth, sea, trees, flowers, dogs, humans – all rushing at you! Sure I was anxious for the friends I left in Pompeii, but I had to admit, this trip was a trip!

But the fate of Olivia, Drusilla and the pups was still uppermost in my mind.

As for Caroline and the Gianni kid, they bickered, they sulked, they yelled at each other – and suddenly, right out of the blue, they were the best of friends, smiling, laughing, talking! There's no logic to human behavior!

We were at a café called Casa del Gatto – hardly a promising name for a restaurant. I looked from one happy, smiling face to another and the events of the morning came flooding back. Olivia and Drusilla and the pups were alone. I had to get back to Pompeii before those weirdos got to them. I sat up and gave Caroline my pleading look, but she was so busy talking to Gianni I could've been juggling oranges and she wouldn't have noticed.

"No, just me" Gianni was saying.

"Only child, huh? I'll bet you usually spend Sundays with your mother."

Gianni sounded amazed. "How you guess this?"

"I'm psychic."

I whimpered a little, but they didn't look down.

"You have, maybe, a boyfriend?" Gianni asked.

Caroline laughed. "What's it to you?"

Gianni's face changed color and he looked down at the table. then Caroline stopped laughing and she looked down at the table too. "Oh, uh – no." She stammered. "No one special."

What was *that* all about?

I wondered if I could thumb a ride back to Pompeii. But dogs are at something of a disadvantage in the thumb department. I flopped down under the table – then my nose twitched. There was something in the air, and it wasn't just the sweet-talk, it was... *Bottiglione's socks*!

I would have known that smell anywhere! He was here! In Ravello!

Suddenly, my every sense was on edge. I wriggled out of the rope round my neck. The kids were too busy gazing into each other's eyes to notice me creeping away from the table. I followed my nose, and the scent led me to a small café on the other side of the square.

It was dark inside after the bright sunlight, and the room appeared to be empty, but the smell of stale wine mixed with Bottiglione's sweat was unmistakable. I heard two muffled voices coming from behind a curtained archway at the far end of the bar.

CHAPTER 12

"How much longer is this going to take?" The hair on my back stood up. It was Monocolo – the thug with the eye-patch and the scar! "Signor Macchiato's patience is growing short."

"There's no rushing it." Bottiglione voice! "Them mutts is cunning. Just when you think you got a couple of 'em cornered, they disappear down an alleyway and you never see 'em again."

Monocolo and Bottiglione! What business did they have together?

"You wouldn't be taking advantage of Signor Macchiato's generosity, would you?" Monocolo sneered.

"Signor!" Bottiglione sounded genuinely wounded by the question.

"Well, hurry it up! I have another little job for you."

A floorboard creaked. I jerked my head up to see Gianni standing next to me. He put a finger to his lips.

"Another job? Certainly!" said Bottiglione. "But we're out of wine. I'll get the waiter."

Gianni and I froze as we heard him get up from the table and shuffle over to the archway. The curtain twitched.

"No more wine" Monocolo said sternly. "I need you sober."

Bottiglione grumbled a bit as he sat back down. Monocolo lowered his voice to a sinister whisper. "This Professor Garibaldi."

"The one who's digging up the Villa?"

"If he finds something of value, anything, we must arrange for him to have – an accident."

There was a long silence. When Bottiglione spoke, his voice was trembling. "I couldn't! Dogs is one thing, but…"

I edged my nose through the curtain and saw Monocolo dump a wad of money onto the table. Bottiglione's fat hand reached for it, but Monocolo produced a knife from out of nowhere and stabbed it into the table. Bottiglione pulled his hand back.

"I'll take care of the details. All you have to do is keep me informed."

Bottiglione nodded. Monocolo pulled the knife out of the table and held the point to Bottiglione's throat. "Understood?"

Suddenly there was a shattering ringing sound – Gianni's cell phone! He fumbled in his pocket to turn it off, but the curtain was thrust aside and Monocolo stood there, glaring at us, the knife in his hand gleaming in the dim light.

CHAPTER 13

CAROLINE'S JOURNAL

Sunday, 17th July

continued

We caught sight of Nero's tail vanishing into a cafe across the square. We didn't want him getting into any more trouble, so Gianni went after him.

I took a deep breath of the clean, fresh air and sipped my coffee thinking how relaxing the day had become and that maybe Gianni wasn't such a pain after all. Then I saw him bolt out of the restaurant with Nero under his arm. He ran to our table.

"We're leaving!"

He shoved Nero at me and pushed my crash helmet onto my head.

"Gianni, if you don't have enough to pay the bill, I can –" He was already revving the scooter.

"*Just get on!*"

"But why the hurry?"

"SUBITO!" He shouted.

Then I saw why the hurry. Across the square, Monocolo was standing in the cafe doorway, with a lethal looking knife in his hand.

"You're right," I said, "forget the bill. We'll send them a check!" I jumped onto the back of the scooter and wedged

Nero between us. Gianni hit the gas and the Vespa surged forward, nearly throwing me off the back.

We tore straight across the middle of the piazza scattering tourists in our wake. I looked back to see Monocolo climbing onto a powerful Italian motorcycle. I could hear his engine start up with a roar as we left the piazza and Gianni headed for the narrow road that wound back down the mountain.

"We'll never get away!" I yelled in his ear. "That thing he's on must have five times the power of this!"

"But only half the – what do you call it?" He wriggled his hand from side to side.

"Maneuverability. *Watch the road*!"

We narrowly missed a car which was coming up the hill.

"I'll head for Minori. We can lose him in the back streets." Gianni shouted.

If we make it that far alive, I thought.

Gianni weaved in and out of the stream of traffic. Drivers yelled at us and blew their horns. We were still well ahead of Monocolo, but then we hit a narrow stretch and got trapped behind a slow-moving truck. All too soon I heard the low-pitched roar of the motorcycle. I looked over my shoulder. He was gaining on us! He disappeared again as we rounded a tight curve, then reappeared, closer this time.

"Hang on!" Gianni yelled. He gunned the Vespa through an impossibly narrow gap between the truck and an oncoming bus. I saw the startled expressions of the passengers as we tore past. The road narrowed again, and this worked to our advantage. Now Monocolo was stuck behind the truck.

A last series of curves, and we sped out onto the coast road. A second of indecision, then Gianni headed east.

I looked behind us. No sign of Monocolo. Traffic on the Amalfi Drive was heavier than on the Ravello road and we soon slowed to a crawl. Gianni snorted with impatience as we dawdled behind another huge bus.

"*Muoviti il culo!*" he shouted at the bus. He glanced over his shoulder to the traffic behind us.

"Monocolo might have gone west instead of east – It's a fifty-fifty chance," I said. Then I heard it – that low powerful sound and it was getting louder.

"*Dio mio*," Gianni muttered under his breath. I looked back. I could see Monocolo now, passing car after car and getting nearer by the second.

"*He's right behind us!*"

Gianni surged forward and we passed the bus on the outside of a blind curve. I clung tightly onto Nero with one hand and even more tightly onto Gianni with the other. We sailed past the bus and struck a clear stretch of road, but Monocolo had also passed the bus and was gaining on us. By the time we rounded the next curve he was pulling alongside us on our left. We were right up against the low stone wall at the cliff's edge.

"I want to talk to you two!" Monocolo shouted. "Slow down before you get us all killed!"

Gianni didn't take his eyes off the road ahead. Nor did he slow down.

Monocolo pulled slightly ahead, then swerved into us.

He was trying to run us off the road!

The Vespa wobbled like crazy. I could see the long drop to our right and the rocks below.

We leant into another curve and Monocolo swung wider and started in towards us again. I thought *this time he'll do it, this time he'll force us over the edge!*

We were neck and neck as we rounded the bend. The sun glinted off a gold tooth in Monocolo's mean smile as he came closer and closer. Then I looked ahead. A fully loaded produce truck was bearing down on us – and Monocolo was directly in its path!

I screamed and Monocolo turned and saw it too! He swerved to the right to avoid the truck. His motorcycle hit the low stone wall and somersaulted, throwing him into the air.

We watched in horror as the motorcycle arced gracefully through the air and plunged into the sea six hundred feet below.

Monocolo followed less gracefully, his arms and legs flailing as he fell.

CHAPTER 14

NERO'S MEMOIRS

Monocolo was no friend of mine, but the image of him going headfirst off the cliff played over and over in my brain – like the time we were watching 'Casablanca' and Fiammetta sat on the 'repeat' button and Elsa said, "Play it, Sam," about a hundred and fifty times.

Gianni drove us back to Pompeii very, very slowly and no one spoke a word the whole way. Caroline clung tightly to me, and I nuzzled into her shoulder to give her what comfort I could.

We parked outside Caroline's hotel and she held me in her arms as we walked into the lobby. Signora Zingarelli's attention was on the TV behind her desk.

On the screen, a crane hauled Monocolo's mangled motorcycle out of the sea while a serious sounding voice described the scene.

"The accident occurred two kilometers west of Minori. So far, there is no trace of the driver of the motorcycle. Police are trying to locate a boy and a girl on a light blue motor scooter who were seen in the vicinity. The girl was carrying a small black dog. Anyone with information concerning…"

Signora Zingarelli switched off the TV and turned towards us. Caroline thrust me at Gianni who shoved me under his shirt. It was all I could do not to yelp.

"Just on our way out" Caroline said as we edged back towards the door and out of the hotel.

I was in total blackout and suffocating!

"We have to go to the police" Caroline said.

"No!"

"But Uncle Tad's life may be in danger!"

"If we tell what we heard, the Professor will close down the excavation!"

"So?"

Gianni sounded very emotional. "So! The Professor works his whole life for this! It will break his heart!"

"*So!*" Caroline said angrily, "What good is some old statue if you're too dead to enjoy it?"

Now Gianni was angry. "Some old statue? *Some old statue*! Haven't you learnt anything since you got here?"

"Yes! I've learnt that you're a pompous, arrogant idiot who thinks a pile of old rocks is more important than people, or dogs, or happiness, or..." She broke off in a sob. It was too much for me. I howled.

Gianni let my head out of his jacket so I could get some air, but no matter how much I wriggled, he didn't put me down! He and Caroline went on arguing. I *had* to get back to Olivia, Drusilla and the pups!

"We have to go to the police. It's our only option" Caroline said.

"No. We have three options" Gianni said calmly. "There are always three options."

"There are?"

"It's a basic law of logic" he said as if talking to an idiot. "One – we tell your uncle. Two – we tell the police. Three – we don't tell anyone."

"Don't tell *anyone?*"

"One – we tell the professor, here is what happens: he fears for the safety of his workers, he closes the dig, Macchiato builds his resort, they confiscate my scooter. Two – we tell the police: I get arrested for reckless driving, they confiscate my scooter..."

"Forget about your stupid scooter!"

"...They find Monocolo's body and we both go to jail until we're sixty-five years old."

"Oh" Caroline said quietly. "I'm starting to see your point."

"Three..."

"We don't tell anyone?"

"Si! We keep on working at the villa. And we keep our ears peeled."

"Eyes. You keep your *eyes* peeled, your *ear* to the ground, your *nose* to the grindstone and your *shoulder* to the wheel."

Gianni sounded totally puzzled. "Che cosa?"

Caroline laughed then she burst into tears again. Gianni let go of me to pull a handkerchief from his pocket and I jumped to the ground. I took a quick look back to the hotel – Signora Zingarelli was at the window with a phone to her ear!

Gianni dried Caroline's eyes. "Please, don't cry Caroline. We *will* find the statue! That will solve everything!"

There was nothing I could do to help, so I took off.

I didn't stop running until I was back in the city. The sun was setting, most of the tourists had gone for the day and the streets were empty.

I skirted the edge of the Grand Palaestra, my nose on the alert for threatening smells. The wind picked up a bit, tossing the tree branches and sending down a fine rain of pine needles, but that was the only sound to be heard. Then the wind changed direction and left me without any warning scent of what might be lurking in the shadows. There was a soft footfall to my left.

I froze, thinking of Bottiglione and Caligula. All the hair on my back stood to attention as the adrenaline coursed through my veins.

A pointed snout emerged from the darkness of a doorway.

"Who's there?" The voice was shaky, hoarse.

It was Agrippina, Caligula's mother – no longer the haughty matriarch; just a frightened old dog in the dark.

"Agrippina! It's me, Nero. Where is everyone?"

She walked haltingly towards me, squinting to make out my face in the half-light.

"Gone. They've all gone."

"Gone? Where?"

"They took all the dogs away in a van."

I swallowed hard. "All of them?"

She nodded.

"But Drusilla and the puppies?"

"They got away just before the van came. Olivia went with them – and that old idiot Augustus too, announcing that they were going to the country just like the Dogs in the Legend."

I pictured the little band setting out into the unknown. None of them had ever been out of the city in their lives. How would they survive in the wild? Augustus, so old and feeble now, and the pups hardly big enough to walk. "Which way did they go?" I said huskily.

"North-west towards Vesuvius."

I looked in the direction of the volcano, massive and mysterious, silhouetted against the dusk sky. A thought occurred to me and I turned back to her. "How come you weren't rounded up with the rest of them?"

Her eyes refused to meet mine. "Caligula came to warn me last night. He told me where to hide." She caught my angry look. "You mustn't judge him too harshly. He's done some terrible things, but he's good to his mother."

Yeah, right, just like the bad guys in the movies. They're always good to their mothers. I nodded farewell, but she didn't look up. She just put her head down and walked back into the shadows.

I turned towards Vesuvius and ran into the night.

CHAPTER 15

CAROLINE'S JOURNAL

Monday, July 18

I showed up early at the dig, trying hard not to dwell on the events of yesterday.

Everyone was already hard at work. Someone had put up a chalkboard with 'Four days to go!' written on it.

Nero has vanished. But fond as I am of him, I can't think about that now. There are more important things to worry about – such as, is Uncle Tad's life in danger?

Gianni took me aside as soon as he caught sight of me and led me into the shadow of the tent. "Anything new?" he asked.

I shook my head. "I kept the TV on all night. Nothing that we don't already know. What about you?"

"There was a report of the accident in the morning papers. They still have not found the body."

"Or us" I said in a whisper. "Just out of interest, how many light blue Vespas are there around here?"

"Hundreds" Gianni said, but he didn't sound very confident. "I see them all the time. Everywhere. Lots of them."

Uncle Tad got back from Naples around nine. He and Fiona spent yesterday looking up all kinds of ancient manuscripts to see if they could throw any new light on Deidamia's whereabouts.

"How was Naples?" I asked him.

"Hot and sticky. If the Museo Archaeologico doesn't install better climate-control in their archive department soon, every manuscript will disintegrate."

"Any luck?"

He shook his head sadly. "I knew it was a long shot, the chance of coming up with anything new at this late date."

I kind of wished I'd gone with them – surely I could have been some help, and I wouldn't now be an accessory after the fact, or whatever they call it in Italy. I found myself wondering what Italian jails were like.

"And how was your day off?" Uncle Tad asked.

"Great!" I said a little too enthusiastically.

"I hope Gianni didn't scare you to death on that infernal scooter of his."

"No" I said, less enthusiastically. "He's – a very careful driver."

Something must've showed in my face. Uncle Tad frowned. "Caroline, are you all right?"

I wanted to tell him everything there and then. About Bottiglione and the dogs, about Monocolo and his threat, about how Gianni and I were practically responsible for his death. But Gianni had sworn me to secrecy, so I just said, "If you find anything, here at the site I mean, you will let me know right away, won't you? Or Gianni! You'll tell us before you tell anyone!"

"Of course." He looked puzzled.

"Promise you'll tell *us*. *Immediately!*"

"I promise. If there's ever anything to tell." He caught

sight of the chalked sign and sighed. "Four more days – I suppose there's still time for a miracle."

I worked all morning, carefully sifting ash that Gianni dug from around a small area of roof tiles. We didn't speak – which was a change – unless there was something about our work we needed to discuss.

Around noon, Jonathan, one of the students approached us, his face red with the heat and running. Gianni leapt to his feet.

"Have they found something?"

"No" Jonathan said. "But there are two men asking for you up at the tent."

"Who are they?"

Jonathan shrugged. "Search me. Never seen them before. But they look like cops."

I clutched Gianni's arm.

"Be chilled" he whispered.

"*Cool*" I whispered back. He gently removed my hand from his arm and we walked up to the tent where Uncle Tad was waiting. A man with sandy hair and wearing a dark, formal looking suit was with him. Uncle Tad hurried to intercept us.

"Why didn't you tell me about this accident?" he asked anxiously. The man put a warning hand on his shoulder and Uncle Tad backed off.

"Detective Sammartini, Commune di Salerno. You are Gianni Roberti?"

"Yes."

The detective led us into the tent.

"You are the owner of a light blue Vespa motor scooter, NA3942?" Gianni nodded. "You were driving east on Route 163 in the vicinity of Minori yesterday at about three p.m.?"

"Yes, we…"

"I believe you witnessed an accident."

"It was mind-blowing!" I said. "Terrifying! Awesome...!"

The detective ignored me. "In your words Signor Roberti."

"The motorcycle was trying to pass me when a truck came the other way."

"You weren't trying to race the motorcycle?"

"A Vespa racing a Ducati?" Gianni asked incredulously.

"As if!" I said with what I hoped was a convincing laugh. Detective Sammartini's face was like stone.

"Why didn't you stop and report the incident?"

Gianni gave me a furtive glance. *He's not very good at this*, I thought. I piped up. "We thought uncle Tad would worry if we were late home."

Uncle Tad stepped forward. "Under the circumstances..." Sammartini raised his hand. Uncle Tad sighed and turned away.

"The motorcycle was one of a fleet owned by Macchiato-Tuttomondo Industries" Sammartini said. "According to Signor Macchiato it was stolen. Do you know anything about that?"

This was a surprise. Gianni and I spoke together. "No!"

CHAPTER 15

"I understand Macchiato-Tuttomondo is financing this archaeological project."

"That's right" Uncle Tad said with a frown.

"An odd coincidence, no?"

Gianni shrugged. I did too. Sammartini took a quick look at his notebook.

"You had a small dog with you."

"He ran away" I said. "All the dogs are being mistreated by…" Sammartini wasn't a bit interested. He produced a card and handed it to Gianni.

"Call me if you think of anything else." He led Uncle Tad outside and I could see them talking a few yards away.

"The Ducati was *stolen*?" I said. "What's up with *that*?"

Gianni scowled – one of his favorite expressions. "Macchiato is lying, to keep himself out of it."

"What now?"

"We return to work! We watch the Professor's front!"

"His *back,* Gianni. We watch his back."

CHAPTER 16

NERO'S MEMOIRS

Signor Umberto placed an enormous dish of spaghetti with meatballs on the table in front of me.

"Buon appetito, Signor Nero," he said with a low bow. I sniffed at the dish.

"What, no parmesan?" I said. Umberto's face fell.

"Forgive me!" He snapped his fingers at Vittorio. "Parmesan for Signor Nero! Now!"

Vittorio started spooning cheese onto my plate. I raised a paw graciously; he'd given me enough. But he wouldn't stop. He just kept piling parmesan onto the plate until it covered my paws! Then it was up over my head, filling up my mouth, my ears, my nose. I was choking on it! With my last breath, I yelped – and woke up under a tree, surrounded by dead leaves.

I remembered now: I'd gathered the leaves into a pile the night before to make a bed.

I'd completely lost my friends' scent, and I was hungry. I wouldn't want to cast any doubt on Augustus's story about the Dogs of Pompeii surviving on rabbits for fourteen thousand dog years, but rabbits must have been a lot slower in those days. The way Augustus tells it, back then, rabbits pretty much hung around waiting to be nabbed by any passing hound. Well, let me tell you, since then the whole dog-rabbit dynamic has changed radically. For a start there aren't as many rabbits. And the ones that are around are a lot more street-savvy than their ancestors. I chased a couple and they seemed to be laughing at me as they vanished into their burrows.

I shook the leaves out of my ears and put my nose to the ground for some hint of Augustus and the others.

I plodded on. There was a farmhouse a little way up the track ahead. It looked run down – some of the roof tiles were missing and the walls could have done with a coat of paint. Still, it was worth a try.

I trotted up to a wide gateway which opened onto a yard. No one was about. I looked over to the house, where smoke was coming out of a chimney near the kitchen door. Maybe there was a Fiammetta-type cook who'd take a shine to me. I put on my most appealing expression (serious and dependable, yet open to harmless fun) and started across the yard.

Suddenly, "AAAAAARRRRRGGGGGHHHHH!!!!!" – or words to that effect.

A Pit Bull Terrier with what looked like three times the normal number of teeth was coming at me full speed across the yard. I decided to get out of there. Fast!

All those teeth were about to sink into my rear end when the Pit Bull jerked back, somersaulted twice and landed flat on his back, all four legs sticking up in the air. He didn't utter a sound.

I went back to him slowly. "You okay?"

"Yeah, I'm fine," he said wearily. "And you're trespassin'!" He staggered upright and shook the dust out of his coat, making a strange jingling sound and

I saw what had brought him up short: a long chain attached to a post near the kitchen door. Next to the post was a dog bowl, half-full of what smelled like tortellini. I tried to keep my eyes from straying to it.

"I didn't mean any harm. I was just looking for – "

"Somethin' to eat?"

"Well, now that you mention it..."

He cocked his muzzle at the dog bowl. "Help yourself, dude. I'm done."

He looked politely the other way as I scoffed every last bit.

"How was it?"

"Mmmm" I said appreciatively. Actually it was a bit overcooked. Fiammetta says eleven minutes for tortellini, no more, no less, and it could have used a bit more parmesan. But I wasn't about to look a Pit Bull in the mouth.

"Sorry about all the snarlin' and barkin' an' stuff " he said affably. "Goes with the job. I'm a guard dog. Name's Samson."

"Nero."

"Nice to meetcha Nero."

"So, what are your duties? You just kinda bark at anyone who goes by?"

He looked indignant. "There's more to it than that! You gotta get the different barks down. Give ya an example."

A little old lady was coming up the track, carrying a basket of groceries. Samson took off to the full extent of his chain, barking furiously.

"ARRGHFFF! ARRGHFFFF! ARRGHFFFFF!!" Which I interpreted to mean, 'keep out'.

The little old lady gave him a cheery smile and waved. "Ciao Samson."

Samson swaggered back to me. I thought a compliment was in order. "Very impressive."

He shrugged modestly. "It's a gift. Ya got it, or ya ain't. How's about you bud? You on the run?"

"How'd you guess?"

"You get to be a shrewd judge of character in my job. Been a few like you passin' by lately." My ears pricked up. "They looked so doggone tired I hardly had the heart to bark at 'em."

"How many?"

"Lessee – big old shaggy dog, nice lookin' female with five teeny tiny pups – and oh yeah" he said with a raised eyebrow, "one real looker – part Greyhound."

I jumped to my feet. "I have to go! Thanks for the Tortellini al Pomodoro Samson!"

"Any time dude."

As I ran off, he inspected his empty dog bowl and said "Tortellini al Pomodoro! Who knew? I thought it was dogfood."

*

My paws were aching by the time a sagging tile roof came into view. It was an abandoned barn, run down and dead looking. Beyond it, the track petered out into a narrow path winding up to the summit of the volcano.

I did a cautious circuit of the building. Doors were hanging off their hinges and there were piles of rubbish and rusty farm equipment everywhere. I kept my nose to the ground, but couldn't pick up any scent.

The inside didn't look too inviting, but I thought I might as well check it out. The door gave an ominous creak as I pushed it open. A skittering sound in the shadows brought me up short. Rats! Then I heard another footfall, high above me. Something heavier than a rat. I looked up. A rickety stair led up to a hayloft and I heard the sound again. Someone or something was up there. I froze.

A pale pink nose poked gingerly over the edge of the loft, followed by a pair of soft brown eyes.

"Nero! Oh Nero, you're here!"

It was Olivia. She pattered gently down the stairs from the hayloft and cautioned me to be quiet. "Drusilla and the pups are napping." I was shocked to see how drawn and tired she looked.

"How long is it since you've eaten?" I asked. Olivia turned away.

"I know, I must look awful." She sat and smoothed back an ear with a graceful movement of her hind leg. "It was a hard journey. We had to take turns carrying the pups."

I pictured the three adults each holding a pup gently by the neck with their jaws, while the remaining two struggled to keep up. Yes, the journey must have been hard. Olivia turned her pretty face back to me.

"It's wonderful to see you, Nero."

"It's good to see you too."

She glanced up the stairs. "I think Augustus's stories about dogs catching rabbits might have been exaggerated."

You bet they were! "So how is Augustus?"

"I think his mind is going" she said quietly. "He goes on and on about how we're fulfilling our destiny as Dogs of Pompeii and how we'll go down in dog history."

"He's too old to deal with all this," I said. "Too set in his ways."

"But we couldn't leave him behind. Those men would have taken him in no time." She sighed. "Dogs like us aren't cut out for this kind of life. We've become too dependent on humans." She sank to the ground despondently. "Nero, what do you think will become of us?"

She looked so helpless. I racked my brain for something encouraging to say. I thought of "Tomorrow is another day" or "You'll never go hungry again", but somehow quoting from a movie it took Fiammetta and me four days to watch seemed a bit irrelevant. Instead I laid my chin on her shoulder in what I hoped was a reassuring gesture.

"Rufus?"

I glanced up. Drusilla was standing above us at the top of the steps.

"Rufus, is that you?"

"No," I said, "It's me, Nero."

Her disappointment was obvious, but being Drusilla, she tried to smile and hurried down the stairs to greet me. "Nero, how good that you're here. But is there any news of –"

I shook my head and she lowered her eyes sadly. The mood was broken as the pups, Primus, Secundus, Tertius, Quartus and Quinta, came tumbling down the steps and licked at me, tails wagging furiously. Drusilla assumed a cheerful tone for their sake.

"Leave Uncle Nero's ears alone! He's come a long way just to see us." Then she became earnest. "Do you think Rufus is – all right?"

I couldn't lie. "I don't know. There's not a single dog left in Pompeii and no one knows where they've gone."

One of the pups dragged a dead rat by the tail across the dirt and presented it to me.

I looked at Olivia, appalled. "You're eating rats now?"

"Necessity my boy, necessity!" Augustus's voice rumbled down from above. He stood proudly at the top of the stairs, but he looked old and frail. "We dogs of Pompeii are survivors! Like our legendary ancestors!"

He started down the stairs, head held high, then he stumbled and fell. We all gasped, but he got to his feet, defying any of us to go to his aid.

"Now that Nero's back in the pack, we'll live here, in the wild, until the time comes for us to return to our home with dignity!" he said.

I regarded the dead rat with a sinking heart.

CHAPTER 17

CAROLINE'S JOURNAL

Tuesday, July 19

2 ½ DAYS TO GO

Never felt so tired! I'll keep this short.

Uncle Tad has decided to concentrate all his efforts on the atrium, which is a sort of courtyard at the very center of a Villa. He and Fiona feel it's logical that such an important work of art as Deidamia would have pride of place there.

So the central area of the site has been excavated to a depth of a few feet. The tops of the stone walls surrounding the atrium are now visible but there's still no sign of the statue.

Those creeps Bottiglione and Luigi were hanging around this afternoon. Clearly Bottiglione is following Monocolo's instructions to keep a sharp eye on Uncle Tad. And Gianni and I are keeping a sharp eye on Bottiglione. Between that and the excavation work we're getting a little cross-eyed.

Bottiglione even had the nerve to ask me if we'd found anything interesting yet. "I didn't know you were so keen on archeology, Signor Bottiglione" I said, all wide-eyed innocence. "If you two are so interested, maybe you'd like to help out?"

Fiona overheard me and thought I'd recruited two more workers. She shoved a bucket into Bottiglione's hands and said "How kind of you! Just keep filling this bucket from that pile of ash and take it to the dump." They had no choice but to start hauling buckets. Gianni and I nearly cracked up, especially when Fiona watched them go and said "A little older than your usual run of student, but we need all the help we can get!"

At least, this way we can keep an eye on them.

We worked until sundown. Uncle Tad came over to us. "Enough! You two need to eat and get some rest."

"It's not late" Gianni said, "we can go on Professor!"
"Not in the dark, you can't."

We closed the site up and dragged our aching feet through the darkened streets of Pompeii. Uncle Tad looked really down.

"Maybe I should close the project."

Gianni opened his mouth to object, but Fiona got in first. "Taddeo!" she said like an angry schoolmarm, "in all the years we've worked together, I've never, *ever* heard you admit defeat!"

"We're getting nowhere" Uncle said quietly. "How do we know the statue is there? No historian ever heard of it, no museum has any record. It all seems hopeless."

"Don't say that, Uncle Tad!" I was close to tears. "You *can't* give up hope! 'Hope is the pillar that holds up the world'!" They all stopped and looked at me. "Pliny the Elder said that just before he died in the eruption of Vesuvius!" Now I felt embarrassed. "I – needed some bedtime reading" I said to Uncle Tad. "I borrowed one your histories of Pompeii."

Gianni smiled broadly at me and tightened his grip on my hand. Uncle Tad smiled too, for the first time that day!

CHAPTER 17

"We'll make an archaeologist of you yet." Then his smile faded. "But with just two days left…"

"And two nights" Fiona said. "We could all work in shifts!"

"No! I couldn't ask that of anyone!"

"I will work nights!" Gianni said.

"So will I!" I said.

Uncle Tad shook his head. "No."

Fiona just said simply "*Yes* Taddeo. And I think you'll find all of your colleagues will agree. Those in favor of working nights?"

We all shouted our approval.

Gianni walked me home. We didn't say much, but we were both thinking a lot – about Monocolo, Macchiato, my Uncle's project – and about Nero.

*

Wednesday July 20

11:50 pm

36 HOURS TO GO

I'm supposed to be resting, but who can sleep? I brought the iPad to the site today to make a few notes. The keys are smudged because my hands are caked with red earth and my nails will never be the same.

The team worked hard all day. Then as the sun went down, a truck arrived with a generator and work lights. We all helped to set them up around the perimeter of the site. They light up the place like day!

Cots have been brought into the tent and the students take turns sleeping for a few hours, then grabbing a cup of coffee and going right on back to the dig. Some continue right through without any sleep at all.

All of us are covered in volcanic ash which really clings to you! But nothing has slowed us down.

We've dug, we've sifted, we've searched holes and troughs, and now, with thirty-six hours to go, we've come up with – exactly nothing.

CHAPTER 18

NERO'S MEMOIRS

I woke with the same empty feeling as when I went to sleep. I could hear the pups whimpering up in the loft. They were hungry too.

As soon as the sun was up, Olivia and I went foraging. We saw a rabbit and gave chase, but it outran us easily. Eventually, we dug up a few turnips from the abandoned farmland near the barn.

"Not turnips again!" Drusilla said. Then she realized how ungrateful this sounded and thanked us.

"Turnips!" Augustus grumbled. "They play havoc with my gas."

"It's the best we could do" Olivia said.

The pups nibbled at them, but with little relish.

There was a dismal silence. My mind wandered and I spoke without thinking. "The average adult dog needs a balanced daily intake of vitamins and nutrients, at least one serving (cupful) of dry food, accompanied by a half serving of protein, such as meat or soy product."

They all stared at me like I was a candidate for a padded kennel. In fact I was quoting from the box label of 'Cane Favorito' dog food which Fiammetta had once given me. She read it to me so often that I memorized it. I'd despised the stuff at the time, but a cupful would sure have been welcome now.

Augustus harrumphed. "I'm not entirely certain what protein is, but I'm sure rabbits have a lot of it!"

"Forget the rabbits" I said wearily. "No dog ever caught a rabbit."

"The ancient Dogs of Pompeii…" Augustus started. I lost it.

"Yeah, yeah, yeah, the dogs caught the rabbits and they made rabbit stew and they trod the grapes and made wine and they sat around smoking cigars!"

Olivia and Drusilla looked on in shocked silence as Augustus drew himself up to his full three feet. "Remember to whom you're speaking!"

"Augustus, we *have to get help*. We have to get back to civilization! We just don't have the instincts to survive in the wild!"

"It's our destiny!" he thundered.

"Destiny!" I barked. "You want us all to starve to death for the sake of posterity? Wake up Augustus! Wake up and smell the coffee!"

"Coffee – wine – cigars" he muttered angrily. "This is the result of associating with humans! You've forgotten what it is to be a dog!"

I tried to reason with him. "We need human help!"

"Humans have driven us to this sorry state! I'd rather die in freedom than live my life on a leash!"

"And what about the pups?"

"Enough Nero! I'm still leader! You will respect my decisions!"

My hackles started to rise and before I knew it, I was baring my teeth.

"No Nero!" Olivia cried. "Augustus is – he's…"

"Quiet Olivia!" Augustus said. "Not another word!" He turned to walk away and suddenly I saw that indeed, Augustus was a very old dog. All the fight went out of me.

"I'm sorry" I called after him.

He didn't turn back, just kept walking to the back of the barn where he slumped down on a pile of straw. There was emotion in his tone when he said, almost to himself: "Nero has become nothing more than a lapdog."

Drusilla gasped. "Augustus, you know I don't like that word! And in front of the pups!"

"It's all right" Olivia said soothingly. "He didn't mean it."

"Yes he did." I said. "Maybe he's right. Maybe I shouldn't have come."

I walked out into the night and sat gazing at the lights in the valley below where life was going on as usual. It didn't take much to see that the problems of a few dogs didn't amount to a hill of beans in this crazy world. I've never actually seen a hill of beans, but I sure could've eaten one now.

After a while, Olivia came and sat next to me.

"How's Augustus?" I asked.

"He's gone to sleep."

"He's an old fool."

"You mustn't mind him, Nero. He's lost everything he cares about. If he loses you too..." Her voice trailed away to silence.

"What's it to him if I stay or go?"

"It means a great deal to him. He just doesn't know how to show it. Talk to him in the morning and I'm sure you'll make it right. But please don't leave. We need you."

I didn't reply. Olivia watched me for some time, waiting for me to give her some assurance that I would stay, but I couldn't.

She got up quietly, padded back into the barn and left me with my thoughts.

*

Between the argument and the turnips I hardly got a wink of sleep. When I did doze off, I dreamt that Caroline and I were sharing a sandwich at Umberto's. I was about to take a bite when Fiammetta came in waving a rolling pin and yelling, "*Not for dogs! Cani non permessi!*" She snatched away the sandwich and poured a bag of "Cane Favorito" dog food into a giant bowl. As soon as the dog food hit the bowl, it turned into rats and they all started chasing me.

Olivia nudged me awake and the early morning sunlight blinded me.

"You were having a bad dream, Nero."

"Rats" I said, with no further explanation.

Drusilla put her head out of the barn door. "The water tank is almost empty."

CHAPTER 18

Now I was fully awake and I could hear Augustus's rumbling, tremulous voice.

"...And the dogs were troubled by the shaking of the earth." I turned to see him sitting in the shade of a tree across the field.

"What's the old fool doing now?"

"He's giving the pups their history lesson" Olivia said. The pups were paying no attention. A couple of them played, tumbling over one another, another scratched lazily, another was fast asleep.

"No birds sang" Augustus went on, dramatically "and the wells and the fountains ran dry."

"We *can't* stay here!" I said. "No matter what Augustus says. There's a guard dog called Samson, half a day downwind. I'm sure he'd give us food if we…" Augustus's lecture rose in volume.

"Unable to wait any longer, the dogs followed the Leader out of the city. They passed a magnificent Villa where stood the beautiful statue of Deidamia, her hand raised in sad and silent farewell to Achilles as he went off to war."

Augustus raised one paw in a gesture of farewell. And suddenly, a flash of memory hit me! *Her hand, raised in farewell...* where had I seen a hand like that?

"And it seemed to the Dogs of Pompeii that Deidamia waved to *them* as they left all that they loved and…"

I bounded over to Augustus. "*Deidamia!*" I barked.

Augustus staggered back against the tree. "Don't do that! You want to give a dog a heart attack?"

"The statue! It's there, isn't it!"

"If you'd paid attention to your history lessons…"

"I have to go back!"

"Back?"

"Back to Pompeii! If I'm in time, we might all be able to go home again!"

Olivia ran to me. "But we need you here!"

Augustus's tone was bitter. "Let him go. He's no longer one of us."

"I'll come back for you! I swear!" I started off at a brisk run. "Go to Samson! Tell him I sent you!"

Olivia raised her head in a desperate howl: "*Neroooooo!*"

CHAPTER 19

CAROLINE'S JOURNAL

Friday, July 22

Deadline day.

The silence of dawn was broken by the rumble of heavy machinery. Everyone on the site looked up to see two enormous bulldozers lumbering over the rise, just beyond the Villa Deidamia site. Their engines cut out and they sat there, waiting, like monstrous beasts of prey.

We all worked on, covered in dirt and sweat. Every now and then, I glanced over to the bell tower of Our Lady of the Rosary in the modern town of Pompeii. The clock read 9:30 – then 10:15 – then 11.

At 11:45, the thunder of a helicopter was heard and Macchiato landed on the edge of the site. As before, the black Mercedes skidded onto the site and two men in black emerged. They took a good look at us all, scrabbling around in the dirt – and laughed.

I noticed that evil little creep Bottiglione lurking by a bulldozer, a grin on his fat red face.

Macchiato emerged from the copter followed by Sofronia. This time she'd dressed for the occasion in designer khaki shorts, designer leather boots, a matching belt with a buckle that I suspected was solid gold and a rhinestone encrusted hardhat – and of course, lots and lots of bangles.

Photographers took pictures as the two men in black plunged two stakes into the ground and stretched a gold ribbon between them. Sofronia took a pair of gold scissors from her dainty purse and posed for the photographers, making sure they had an uninterrupted view of her cleavage.

Macchiato waved his hand and the bulldozers started up. The air was filled with diesel fumes and the din of revving motors. The 'dozers rocked back and forth as if eager to mow down anything that stood in their path.

I glanced at the clock tower.

11:58.

Uncle Tad went to the edge of the site and blew a whistle. A groan of dismay went up from all the workers and slowly, reluctantly, we all walked off the site.

The area stood empty for the first time since Uncle Tad and his team had broken ground six months earlier. The Macchiato entourage stood at one end and the archaeologists at the other, like opposing armies on a battlefield.

The bell of Our Lady of the Rosary started to strike the noon hour. Sofronia stepped forward, ready to cut the ribbon on the final stroke of twelve.

One …

Fiona, usually such a tower of strength, was in tears and a couple of the students were too. But all that could be heard above the roar of the bulldozers was the tolling of the bell.

Two – three…

Suddenly, from out of nowhere, a streak of black fur headed for the dig site. There was a piercing shriek from Sofronia as the streak hurtled between her ankles and knocked her flat on her khaki ass.

Four…

CHAPTER 19

"Nero!" Gianni and I yelled simultaneously. He ignored us and ran to the far end of the site and started digging furiously, throwing huge quantities of earth high into the air.

Five …

Bottiglione unhitched a rope from his belt and started towards Nero, but he caught my eye and thought better of it. No one else moved. They all seemed transfixed by the sight of this small black dog intent on finding – *what?*

Six…

Gianni picked up a spade and ran to Nero and started digging right beside him. He turned round to Uncle Tad and yelled, "Dig! Dig!"

Seven…

Uncle Tad grabbed a spade and joined in. I tried to get Nero out of the way – but he just wriggled out of my grasp and went on digging.

Eight… Nine…

A bronze hand appeared out of the earth. Nero dug round it, determined to expose as much of it as possible.

Ten…

Uncle Tad fell to the ground and started scooping up earth with his bare hands. "*We've found her!*" he yelled. "*We've found Deidamia!*"

Eleven…

Uncle Tad and Gianni threw down their spades and started hooting and hollering like it was Super Bowl Sunday. They were dancing around and hugging each other and crying, and hugging Nero, whose tail wagged so hard I thought it would fall off.

Twelve.

Signor Macchiato strode across to us, stepping over Sofronia without a glance.

Uncle Tad proudly indicated the bronze hand. "This discovery is clear evidence that we're on a site of great historical importance!"

"SPLANAZINI!" Macchiato yelled.

Spalanzini stumbled forward and fumbled through the pages of the contract. He read: "If a bona fide historical artifact is found within the agreed period…"

Macchiato snatched the papers from him, then pointed his cigar in Uncle Tad's face. "It's not over yet" he said menacingly. "My resort is going to open and open on time. Even if it's over someone's dead body!"

With that he turned on his heel and strode to the helicopter, ignoring Sofronia, who was busy dusting her backside. She ran after him as fast as her boots could carry her.

Uncle Tad was beaming the broadest smile I've ever seen and all the crew shook his hand and slapped him on the back. Then Fiona kissed him on the cheek.

It's the first time I've ever seen a grown man blush!

CHAPTER 20

NERO'S MEMOIRS

That night there was a celebration dinner at Umberto's and I was guest of honor! All the geeks were there. The professor toasted me as the first dog in history to make a major archaeological discovery.

"Why didn't I think of it before? It's perfectly logical for a statue in an attitude of greeting or farewell to be placed at the entrance to the house. And it took Nero to figure it out for me!"

Fiammetta came out of the kitchen to greet me. She was crying and wiping her eyes on a dish towel and said I was like Humphrey Bogart just back from winning World War Two (whatever that is) single handed. It was nice to be compared to my hero.

Signor Umberto served dinner and brought a large steak to the table. He set it down in front of Caroline who said "No, the steak is for Nero."

I'll never forget the look on Umberto's face as he very reluctantly put the plate on the floor for me. I took a couple of bites, then I was overcome with guilt as I thought of Olivia, Drusilla and the pups and Augustus. I stopped eating and looked up at Caroline.

"What's the matter, Nero? Don't you like it?"

Of course I liked it, but the thought of my starving friends wouldn't allow me to swallow a bite.

"Never mind," she said. "I'll see that you eat whatever you like, whenever you like from now on." And with that, she reached into her bag, saying, "I have a little present for you." She took out a collar and a leash!

I thought of turning tail and running, but Gianni held me firmly as she put the collar around my neck.

"See? It has a little tag with your name on it." They attached the leash to the collar and I was trapped.

After dinner, Caroline took me back to her hotel. Signora Zingarelli gave her special permission to have a dog in her room. And if the collar and leash weren't undignified enough, that night Caroline gave me a – *bath*.

I don't think I've ever been so embarrassed in my life! What is it with humans and baths? I've never had a problem with the way dogs smell. Sometimes it's the best way to tell friend from foe. If humans smelled like dogs, maybe they could sort out the good guys from the bad more easily.

Thrashing about in the tub, I did what I usually do when I'm embarrassed – I howled. Signora Zingarelli came by to see if I was in pain. Well, I certainly *was*!

With all my struggling to get out of the water, Caroline got as wet as I was. "Now I know what soap tastes like" she said, laughing. I thought it was no laughing matter.

When I was dry, she locked the door and went to bed. I was a prisoner. I whimpered for a while, but Caroline had no real understanding of why I was unhappy, so she merely stroked my head, and went to sleep.

When I finally got to sleep, I dreamt – as all dogs do. But not of food, or tennis balls, or chasing cats – I dreamt of Olivia.

CHAPTER 21

CAROLINE'S JOURNAL

Umberto's Café

Friday, 29th July

The last week has been one of the happiest and busiest of my life! It took four whole days to free Deidamia from the earth and volcanic ash surrounding her, and another whole day to lift her gently onto a trailer. From there, she was taken to the onsite laboratory, where Gianni and Uncle Tad hosed her down carefully to wash the dirt of two thousand years off her. She really is the most beautiful thing I've ever seen.

She has tightly curled ringlets and a kind of crown around her hair. The folds of her gown are so detailed they might be real silk instead of bronze. And the expression on her face is one of unbelievable sadness – after all, she is saying goodbye to Achilles! Her left hand rests on her heart as if she's incredibly sad, and her right is raised high, waving farewell.

There's been no sign of Macchiato or any of his heavies, but, mindful of the threats we overheard that Sunday in Ravello, a few of the students we trust with our secret information have taken it in shifts to guard both the statue and Uncle Tad.

Today is the big day when they move the statue to the Archaeological Museum in Naples.

Uncle Tad looks ten years younger just knowing he can continue his work on the villa. The only long face in the whole of Pompeii is Nero's. For some reason, he just sits and mopes, as he's doing right now by my table. I keep him on the leash at all times. I haven't seen him around, but Bottiglione must have been up to his dog-catching dirty work, because there's not a dog left anywhere in Pompeii. Except Nero. And whatever it takes, I'll protect him.

CHAPTER 22

NERO'S MEMOIRS

My days of captivity were the unhappiest I can remember. Sure I had all the care and attention any dog would want, and the human lavishing her affection on me was Caroline. It should've been canine heaven – but my thoughts were with my exiled friends. I wanted to prove to Augustus that I was not the lapdog he thought I was – that I could lead him and Olivia and Drusilla and the pups back into Pompeii, back to our rightful home. But that was not to be, not yet.

Every day, Caroline and I walked through the city together, dodging the tourists, on our way to the dig. I strained on my leash to search corners and shadows, hoping for a glimpse of an old friend, but there was no sign of the Dogs of Pompeii. They had all gone. I felt an ache deep inside that I'd never known before.

The geeks lifted the statue out of the ground and washed her – they even bathe statues! I wish Augustus could've been there to see her before they packed her away. He, of all dogs, would've been overjoyed to see the object of his history lessons in the flesh – or in the bronze.

As I watched the professor and his team at work, I started to understand why the geeks are so driven. Archaeology is not just about digging up old junk, it's about humans and their history and their legends and their dreams. It's about the road you've taken to where you're at now. And somehow, it's about the road ahead too. For the first time, I saw what was so important about Augustus's history lessons – the ones I never paid any attention to. And just as we dogs should never forget our heritage, neither should humans. If more people did a bit of digging, they might learn more about themselves. How's that for some deep thinking?

As they put the statue into the box, Caroline said, "Isn't she beautiful, Nero?"

I had to admit it wasn't the kinda thing you'd raise your hind leg at. I guess that's the power of art that the Professor's always talking about.

A few drops of water still glistened on Deidamia's bronze cheeks, like the tears she shed as she saw Achilles off to the Trojan war. Call me crazy, but the look in her eyes reminded me of Olivia the day I left her and the other dogs in the country. I turned from Deidamia to Caroline to Gianni to the Professor, and while I was happy for them, I wondered if Olivia would ever forgive me for leaving. How could I make her understand that what I did was as much for my canine friends as for the humans?

I strained at my leash as the box was loaded onto the professor's truck and Caroline must've misinterpreted this, because she sighed and said, "If you must, you must. But stay close to me." She unclipped the leash.

Freedom!

For a moment, I stood rooted to the spot, too surprised to move.

Fiona joined the Professor as he climbed into the truck. "I wish you'd let me come with you. It's a long drive to Naples."

The Professor patted her cheek. "You need to take a break. I'll be back for supper." And he started the engine.

Fiona returned to where Gianni, Caroline and I were standing. "He shouldn't go alone."

The Professor drove off.

"I will look after him!" Gianni said, and he mounted his motor scooter and kicked it into life. It was now or never. I bounded across the site and leapt onto the foot board. Caroline yelled after me.

"Nero! Come back here!"

Gianni just laughed. "It's okay. Nero's coming to Naples with me!"

We took the road west past the Villa dei Misteri and headed out into open country and onto the Naples autostrada. It was great to be back on Gianni's Vespa, with the wind whistling through my fur and all the country smells whirling around my head. Vesuvius was to our right in the distance – just a little closer and I could make a break for it and get back to my friends.

As we rounded a curve just outside Torre del Greco we were forced to slow down. A couple of gorilla-like road workers were lounging against a barrier at the side of the road. As the Professor's truck approached, they moved the barrier across the highway and waved him onto a narrow, dusty side road. Gianni slowed down to read out the sign: "'Diversione!' We have to take a detour, Nero" he said impatiently. "Our trip to Naples will take longer than we thought."

He turned the scooter towards the side road, but the gorillas dragged the barrier across it, blocking our way. He skidded to a stop. "Hey, I need to go that way!"

One of the gorillas came lumbering over. "Sorry kid, road's closed."

"But I'm with that truck!"

The guy shrugged. "Too bad. Road works."

Something didn't add up – there were only two of these guys and they weren't doing any work as far as I could see.

Gianni lost his temper. "You haven't started work yet! Let me through!"

The guy sneered. "You gotta problem, file a complaint."

Gianni muttered "Hang on Nero!" He skidded round the side of the barricade and we took off like a rocket. The gorillas shouted at Gianni and he yelled a couple of words back over his shoulder. I'm not sure what they meant, but the workers sure knew and they looked pretty mad. They started to run after us, but it was no use. We were away in a cloud of dust. I was proud of Gianni – Bogart himself couldn't have done any better.

We rounded a corner and there, up ahead, was the Professor's truck. It was over on the side of the dusty road, its front end in a ditch. The Professor was sitting on the ground looking dazed.

Gianni braked. "Professor!" He left his scooter in the middle of the road and we ran to the Professor. I saw to my horror that there was blood on his head and one arm hung limp at his side. Then I looked at the truck. The truck was empty!

"Your arm!" Gianni said. He touched it and the Professor cried out in pain. "I think it's broken!"

"They've taken the statue" The Professor said between clenched teeth. Gianni leapt to his feet.

"Nero, stay here! Guard the Professor!" He ran back to his scooter and started it up. "I'm going after them!"

"Gianni, no!" called the Professor. "Get the police!"

But Gianni was off, his cell phone to his ear.

CHAPTER 23

CAROLINE'S JOURNAL

Friday, 29th July

continued

Gianni sounded frantic on the phone. He told me to call an ambulance for the Professor, he was going after the crooks. I begged him not to follow them, but begging Gianni to do *anything* except what *he* wants to do is pointless.

I grabbed Fiona and we ran to where her mini was parked. She was in such a state, I wasn't sure if she could drive, but she got a grip on herself, swept the hair back out of her eyes, and headed out on the Naples highway while I called the emergency number.

Needless to say, there was no sign of the road workers Gianni told me about, or their phony detour.

We got Uncle Tad to the hospital and they set his arm. Fiona fussed – and boy, can she fuss! And the more she fusses, the more Scottish she gets! The nurse assured her he would live and she calmed down a bit and switched her concern to archaeology in general. "What a catastrophe for history – for *posterity*!" I gave her a couple of aspirin – she needed them more than Uncle Tad.

Detective Sammartini was shown in and started to ask questions.

"I didn't see the men clearly" Uncle Tad explained. "They were wearing masks. One of my students went after them."

My cell phone buzzed. It was Gianni. "Don't say anything to anyone!" he said, before I even spoke.

Sammartini was right by my shoulder. "Would that student happen to be your friend, Gianni Roberti?"

"Uh – yes, but he lost them" I lied. Sammartini kept his eyes fixed on me for a long moment. I don't think he believed a word I said. But he turned back to Uncle Tad and I slipped out into the corridor. Nero followed. He hadn't left my heels since we brought Uncle Tad back to Pompeii.

"Caroline, listen" Gianni said in a hoarse whisper, "I tailed them to an old metal foundry near the Port of Torre del Greco. They took the statue inside."

"Why can't I just tell the police that's where you are?"

"Do you know how long it takes to get a search warrant? Macchiato could get the statue out of the country by tonight! Or worse, he could destroy it! No! Ho un piano!"

I've come to learn that the three scariest words in the Italian language when uttered by Gianni are 'Ho un piano' – 'I have a plan'. As he outlined his plan, I wondered if insanity ran in his family.

Suddenly Sammartini was at my side. "Do you have anything to add Signorina?" I flipped my phone shut looking as guilty as I actually felt.

"Nope" I said with a shaky smile.

I didn't exhale until Sammartini got into the elevator at the end of the corridor. Then I went back to Uncle Tad and told him I needed a nap.

"You deserve one" he said. "Nero?" Nero's ears pricked up. "Look after my niece." Nero cocked his head to one side as if he understood every word.

CHAPTER 23

Fiona didn't need to be asked twice to stay with Uncle Tad. She pulled a chair close to his bed and read to him from an old copy of Archaeology Today. Not surprisingly, the article she chose dealt with the marriage rites of the ancient Etruscans.

CHAPTER 24

NERO'S MEMOIRS

Again, I was the victim of divided loyalties. I owed so much to my human friends that I felt I couldn't desert them now when they needed me. But what about my exiled friends?

As soon as it was dark, I followed Caroline into Pompeii. Gianni had instructed her to wait for him on Via della Tombe. The avenue is lined with the tombs of ancient Romans and Caroline was very nervous – a dog can sense these things.

A dark figure dressed entirely in black with a mask over his whole face appeared from behind a tomb. Caroline cried out. Then we heard Gianni's laugh and he took off the mask.

"You fear seeing a ghost maybe?" he said.

"You fear getting a black eye?"

Then Gianni took a good look at her. "What is this jacket with the big letters? I said wear something black!"

"Surprising as it may seem" Caroline said angrily, "I don't own anything black! This is my dad's team jacket. I brought it on the trip for luck – which I have a feeling we're going to need."

Gianni pointed at the bright lettering on the back of the jacket. "What is this 'Princeton'?"

"It's a place for *smart* students!" she said.

*

We rode to Torre del Greco and stopped in an alley in a deserted section of the old port. Most of the streetlights were out, so you could hardly see a thing.

Gianni got off the scooter. "This is it. The metal foundry."

"Now what?" Caroline asked.

"Simple" Gianni said. "We break in, we get the statue, we call my friend Angelo who has a pickup truck, we load the statue onto the truck, we take it back to Pompeii. Simple."

I started to wonder if this kid was playing with a full deck.

"Just like that?" Caroline asked. "What if there's a security system?"

Gianni sighed. "This place has been derelict for years! If there is an alarm it won't be working." He crouched down by me. "Nero, stay! Keep watch! You see anyone, bark! Loud!" He looked up at Caroline. "You think he understands?"

What's to understand? Someone comes, I bark. It ain't rocket science.

He took a tire iron from his saddle bag and he and Caroline started towards the foundry. I heard a crack of splintering wood followed by the creak of a hinge – they were in!

It was too chilly just to stand about, so I decided a quick patrol around the perimeter of the building might be smart. You never know when you might be attacked from the rear – something Gianni was clearly unprepared for. He had guts, sure, but he'd never get my vote as alpha dog.

I made a circuit of the entire building, leaving a few messages along the way to make sure no one thought the place was unprotected.

I'd just got back to the front when I heard a vehicle approaching. The vehicle, a little green van, went on up the street.

A little green van!

I followed it as stealthily as I could. The van creaked to a halt outside a dingy, closed up pasta factory that hadn't seen a noodle in years. The driver killed the motor and got out. Bottiglione!

Luigi followed and opened the back doors of the van. It was piled high with sacks which the two of them started to unload. On the side of one of the sacks I recognized an all-too-familiar picture – a dog with a psychotic smile drooling over a bowl of dog food – Cane Favorito dog food!

"These mutts never had it so good" Bottiglione said. "They should go down on their bony little knees and thank us."

Luigi looked puzzled. "I didn't know dogs had knees." Bottiglione swiped him across the head.

"Just unload the chow! My pal Nunzio over at Cane Favorito wants 'em all fattened up."

Luigi dropped his sack and put a hand to his mouth. "Do you have to talk about it Botti?"

"Bottiglione! Signor Bottiglione!"

"Makes my stomach turn when I thinka turnin' dogs into –" Luigi gulped, "– dog food."

Bottiglione laughed. "Hey, it's a dog-eat-dog world, ain't it?"

Luigi looked as if he might throw up. Bottiglione slapped him on the back, which didn't help.

"Just remember we're gettin' fifteen Euros a dog! Multiply *that* by a couple hundred mutts!"

Luigi tried with both hands, but couldn't. Bottiglione pushed him towards a shabby wooden door.

"Move! We got twenty-four hours to get 'em over to the dog food factory – all nice and plump and juicy!"

Luigi turned white and heaved a couple of times. Bottiglione turned a key in the padlock at the door. Instantly, there was a sound of yelping, barking!

"SHUDDUP YA MUTTS!" Bottiglione yelled. Then the two of them dragged sacks of dog food inside and shut the door.

The dogs were alive! My friends were alive! But only for another twenty-four hours! I had to do something – but what? What would Bogie do? He'd get backup! Yeah, backup!

I ran back towards the metal foundry and skidded to a halt when I saw a big black car parked outside – a big black car that wasn't there when I left. Its motor was purring quietly, its doors were open and a shadowy figure sat in the driver's seat.

CHAPTER 24

The foundry door opened. I stayed out of sight and watched as a tall figure emerged from the foundry carrying something. The figure looked familiar. A streetlight lit his scarred face.

Monocolo!

And the something he was carrying was *Caroline!*

Before I could think about launching an attack, Monocolo dumped her on the back seat of the car and jumped in.

"Move! We're takin' her to Medea!"

With a squeal of tires, the car took off. I raced after them, but it was no use – dogpower is no match for horsepower.

Where was Gianni? Why wasn't Mr Smartguy on top of this? I ran back to the open foundry door and put my nose inside. Yep, there was Gianni's scent. But there was something else, too – a sickly, sweet-sour smell I couldn't identify.

I crept in and stumbled over something – Gianni! He was stretched out on the concrete floor. He looked dead – but no, he was breathing. I barked.

"GET UP! GET UP!"

He didn't move. I tugged at his jacket, but he was out for the count. Where was that sickly smell coming from? A bottle and a crumpled rag lay beside his face. I sniffed at the bottle and gagged. Gianni's prone figure seemed to undulate before my eyes, then everything went black and I felt myself spiraling downwards into a bottomless pit.

CHAPTER 25

CAROLINE'S JOURNAL

Motor Yacht 'Medea'

Amalfi Bay.

Friday night, 29th July (I think)

I'm writing this on yacht stationery because that's where I am – 'guest' of Signor Macchiato. And I use the term 'guest' loosely. But I'm telling it all back to front, so let me start from the beginning.

Gianni's great 'plan' was to get the statue back. Simple, huh? Anyway, off we went on his Vespa, all dressed in black – except me, because black is out this year. Nero came along as guard dog. Gianni was convinced the foundry was deserted. Did he get that wrong, or what!

Gianni got the side door open with a tire lever and we went inside. It was very, *very* dark. He had a small flashlight which wasn't much help and as we edged across the concrete floor, we stumbled into the crate containing the statue.

Gianni used the lever to pry the boards off the front and there was Deidamia, gleaming a dull green in the beam of his flashlight.

We heaved at the statue, but it wouldn't budge.

"For a size six, this girl weighs a ton!" I said.

Gianni scratched his head. "We need a jack. And something with wheels. And some rope. And some planks.

And –"

"Six other people?" I suggested.

"Just stay here."

"By *myself?*"

Gianni put his hand on my shoulder. "There's nothing to be afraid of Caroline, I'm here."

Why didn't this reassure me the way it should have? He gave me the tire iron and took the flashlight leaving me in total darkness. The beam vanished as he rounded a corner. I waited there for what seemed like eternity. Nothing. Not a sound. Some date this was turning out to be.

Someone stepped on something, very close to me. I gasped and turned, but there was only impenetrable darkness.

"Gianni? Is that you?"

Good question I thought. Who else would it be? Suddenly a glaring light was switched on, right in my face! Maybe Gianni had found a bigger flashlight. The light came closer. I stepped back and crashed into the open crate. My first thought was for the statue – what if she fell! I grabbed Deidamia around her slender waist to steady her.

"Gianni! Help me!" No answer. I turned back into the glare of the light and now, reflected in the glow, was a familiar face with a familiar eye-patch and a familiar scar.

Monocolo!

My first thought was, "He's not dead – Gianni and I won't have to go to jail after all." My second thought was, "It doesn't matter, because he's going to kill us."

I might've cried out, I don't remember. What I do remember is the overpowering smell of chloroform as

CHAPTER 25

Monocolo pushed a soaked rag into my face. And then, as they say in the classics, I knew no more.

So here I am on Macchiato's palatial yacht. As far as I can tell, I'm being held hostage – even though the smarmy Macchiato insists I'm his 'dinner guest'. Great way to invite a girl to dinner!

Monocolo is the only one who talks to me, but his English is terrible, and I've a feeling it's better if they don't know I understand Italian.

Soon as the chloroform wore off and I stopped throwing up, I looked into the possibilities of escape, but this cabin is really low down in the boat (I think I'm in the crew's quarters) and the portholes are too small to squeeze through, even if I started Jenny Craig right away.

They took my cell phone away, which is a real bummer – it's like losing both hands. But even if I had it, who would I call? Mom? She'd want to call the Defense Department and have them send in a destroyer or something. Plus, there'd be a huge lecture along the lines of, 'This is what comes of associating with the wrong sort of Italian boys.'

What about my best friend Didi Carr? She'd only say, 'You're a hostage? How cool is that!' Then she'd get another call and forget to call me back.

Gianni? 'Voicemail' is a foreign word to him, so he wouldn't check in until I was... well, whatever they plan to do with me. Speaking of Gianni, what happened to him? I'm pretty sure he isn't on the yacht. I just hope he's okay. Wherever he is.

CHAPTER 26

NERO'S MEMOIRS

I was in Rick's café in Casablanca, Sam was playing the piano and I was eating Pizza Napoletana.

I opened my eyes. I was flat on my back and sick to my stomach. I struggled up onto all fours, and fell over Gianni who was still out cold.

I tugged at his jacket – nothing. I nipped his finger – nothing. I licked his face. He didn't open his eyes, but he smiled and said a dreamy "Caroline."

Gimme a break.

I barked into his ear, loud as I could. His eyes jerked open and he sat up.

"*Caroline!*"

I tugged at a piece of paper stuffed into the pocket of his jacket. He snatched it from me and read it out loud.

"DO NOT CONTACT THE POLICE OR YOU WILL NEVER SEE THE GIRL AGAIN."

He staggered his feet. "Where have they taken her?"

"Medea" I barked! "They've taken her to some dame called Medea!"

"Nero quiet! My head aches!"

I kept barking. "*Medea* for cryin' out loud! What, am I talkin' Greek?"

"*Quiet Nero!* I must think!"

Gianni stumbled out of the foundry and into the street.

"Nero, where's Caroline? Which way did they go?"

I sniffed harder than I've ever sniffed, but that sickly smell was clogging my brain and I couldn't get a fix on Caroline's scent. I led Gianni to where the big black car had been. There were skid marks on the cobblestones.

In the movies, the hero always follows tire tracks like these directly to the house where the girl is being held prisoner, but deep down I had a feeling that wouldn't work for us.

Gianni looked up and down the street. I gave it one more try.

"MEDEA! MEDEA!" I barked.

"*Basta!*" he yelled at me.

Thousands of years of interaction between man and dog, and *still* they can't understand us!

"Detective Sammartini – I must call Detective Sammartini" he muttered. He fumbled in his pocket and pulled out a small white card. As he reached for his cell phone, he dropped the card and it fluttered to the sidewalk – right next to a gleaming, silvery object.

"It's a cigarette lighter!"

This kid had amazing powers of deduction.

"There's something engraved on the side." He stumbled over to a street lamp, and held the silver lighter under it.

CHAPTER 26

"Medea!"

Bingo!

He secured me between his feet on the scooter and we zoomed off on the cliff road. The rushing wind cleared my brain, but my sense of smell had definitely taken a nosedive since I was knocked out. I just hoped it wasn't permanent.

Gianni parked high on a cliff overlooking the bay of Amalfi. Then he took a pair of binoculars from the bag and scanned the bay.

The lights of millionaires' boats glittered in the crisp night air.

"There!" Gianni said triumphantly. "Macchiato's floating palace, the yacht Medea! That's where they've taken Caroline!"

Gianni was all for swimming out there and rescuing her. Which movie did he see *that* in? But he figured he'd be up against Macchiato's heavies. So there was nothing to do but wait and see what happened next. He sat on a rock, his binoculars trained steadily on the yacht. I sat next to him – and we waited.

"They're having some sort of dinner party on deck. Good name for the yacht of a crook" Gianni said. "Medea. It's an old Greek story about this woman who murders her children."

Gimme Lassie any day!

Suddenly Gianni jumped to his feet. "Look! There's something hanging out of one of the portholes, right down near the water. It has big lettering: P – R – I – N – C... *It's Caroline's jacket!* She's signaling! She must be a prisoner in that cabin!" Then he tilted the binoculars to another angle and gasped.

"*Monocolo! He's alive!*"

Well, I coulda told him that.

"He's getting into a launch! He's bringing the dinner guests ashore! Come on!"

We got back onto the scooter. I hated the saddle bag, but given the speed we were going, I guess it was safer than the footboard. We drove down to the marina.

Gianni parked and darted into the shadows. He said 'shh' and 'quiet' and 'not a sound'. Hey, I wasn't saying a word!

Monocolo pulled the launch up to the pier, tied it up and helped a few rich looking swells out of it. They walked right past us saying a bunch of things which I didn't understand, though Gianni seemed to get it all.

"...piece of the action when he lays the foundation stone of the casino..."

"...smart guy, that Macchiato..."

"...call my investment broker first thing..."

Then Monocolo walked by – or I should say, staggered by. He'd obviously had a few. He held a large key ring in his hand which jingled as he swayed down the pier.

"I'll bet those keys open every cabin on the yacht" Gianni said, and we followed Monocolo, keeping in the shadows. He went into a pretty low looking dive with a flickering neon sign over the door. Gianni told me what it said: 'Elefante Rosa.'

CHAPTER 26

He scrabbled about in his saddle bag and pulled out a baseball cap which he shoved on his head and a pair of very dark glasses – then a small tube of something which he squeezed onto his upper lip. He turned to me.

"Be strong Nero."

I had no idea what he was talking about until – he yanked a bunch of hair from my tail. Apart from the indignity, it was all I could do not to yelp out loud.

Gianni stuck the hair onto his upper lip and he looked like –well, a kid in sunglasses and a baseball cap with dog hair on his lip. But I guess to him it was disguise. I thought, *this kid's seen more movies than I have.*

"Stay here Nero" he said as he started for the dive.

Are you kidding? The kid needed all the help he could get. I followed at a discreet distance.

As Gianni opened the door, a cloud of cigarette smoke hit us like a wall. Gianni coughed. I sneezed. Then I darted between his feet and crept into a dark corner, which wasn't hard. *All* the corners in this joint were dark.

I figured this was one of those gin joints Bogie talked about. But Rick's Cafe Americain it wasn't.

Gianni took one step forward and fell flat on his face.

"Watch where you're goin'" a waiter said and stepped over him.

Gianni raised the sunglasses so he could see what he was doing and as I heard his intake of breath, I saw what he saw: across the room, sitting on a table and gleaming in the dim light was – the key ring. Unfortunately, the guy sitting *at* the table was Monocolo. In front of him was an empty glass. A waiter picket up the empty and slopped down a full one. Boy, I thought, these waiters wouldn't last five seconds at Umberto's.

Monocolo picked up the glass and drained it in one gulp. He slammed the glass back on the table, but his head stayed in the tossed back position. He uttered a faint snore. This was our chance.

Gianni scrambled to his feet and crept to Monocolo's table. He reached out. His fingers touched the key ring, then – THUNK! Monocolo's knife slammed into the center of the ring nearly amputating a couple of Gianni's fingers. To the kid's credit, he didn't flinch. Monocolo narrowed his one bleary eye.

"Don't I know you?"

"No!" said Gianni. "Never saw you before!"

"You sure?"

"Sure! I never forget an eye... *A face!*"

Monocolo pulled him down into the chair next to him. "Buy you a drink?" he slurred. "Got a bonus from the boss tonight. Whad'll it be?"

"Uh – Chinotto."

Monocolo laughed a gravelly laugh and muttered something to the waiter.

I don't know what kind of Chinotto they served in this gin joint, but it sure didn't agree with Gianni. Before long there was a row of empty glasses on the table and Gianni was singing some old Italian folk song. His glasses were crooked – and so was his mustache!

CHAPTER 26

Monocolo shoved a cigarette into his mouth. "Hey kid, gotta light?"

"Yeah sure!" Gianni said with a silly smile. He dragged the cigarette lighter out of his pocket and flicked it open. Monocolo's eye opened wide and suddenly he was stone cold sober.

"*Medea!*" He tore Gianni's cap and glasses off – the mustache fell off by itself. "You're the kid nearly killed me!" He pulled the knife from the table and stuck it against Gianni's ribs. "Gettup. We're takin' a little walk."

He snatched the key ring from the table and frogmarched Gianni to the door. I had to do something! What would Bogie do….? He'd do that coat thing he did in the movie about the black bird!

I leapt onto a chair and launched myself at Monocolo's back. I got the collar of his coat firmly in my jaws and dropped to the ground hauling the coat halfway down Monocolo's body, trapping his arms. He dropped the knife and the keys. As the key ring fell, I jumped up and grabbed it in my teeth – all that tennis ball training had come in handy!

As I ran out the door, I heard Monocolo yell "Stop that dog!" I also heard Gianni yell "I'll drink to that", and a solid *clunk* as he hit the floor.

Monocolo was pretty fast on his feet for a drunken slob, but I made it to the end of the pier. The Medea launch was moored right there. I bounded into it and Monocolo jumped in right after me. He came at me slowly with the knife. I backed up snarling.

"Good dog, give Uncle Monocolo the keys."

This guy was as shallow as an empty water bowl.

"Gimme the goddam keys!" He threw the knife which missed me by a whisker.

I was at the very back of the boat – there was nowhere to go. Until this moment, 'dog paddle' was only a vague term to me. Now it was sink or swim.

The keys clenched firmly in my jaws, I jumped into the icy water. I heard Monocolo belly-flop into the water, then he said "Merda! I forgot! I can't swim!"

I struck out across the cold black water toward the distant lights of the 'Medea'.

CHAPTER 27

CAROLINE'S JOURNAL

Motor Yacht 'Medea'

Amalfi Bay

same night

Dinner was fine if your idea of a good time is listening to five Italian businessmen conniving.

Macchiato's dining room, or whatever you call it on a yacht, was bigger than your average New Jersey apartment. Doors at either end were guarded by Macchiato's thugs, just in case I tried to make a break for it.

I thought I'd go out of my mind with boredom, and Sofronia was nearly asleep in the soup, but I forced myself to pay attention in case I learned something useful. Of course I didn't let on that I understand Italian – that way they weren't too careful about what they said in front of me.

Seems they're holding me for 'insurance', just in case they can't find a loophole in the rules that allow Uncle Tad to excavate the Villa.

Spalanzini the lawyer went through the contract point by point and every time Signor Macchiato raised an objection Spalanzini shot it down – he almost seemed to take a perverse pleasure in getting Signor Macchiato mad.

"Mi dispiace Signor Macchiato, the clause is clear-cut." He cleared his throat and read: "If some historical artifact is..."

Historical artifact! Historical artifact!" Macchiato exploded. "The only historical artifact around here is you!"

"Which would make me fully protected by the terms of this contract," Spalanzini commented dryly. I almost burst out laughing, then remembered I wasn't supposed to know what was going on.

Signor Macchiato's face creased in a smug smile. "No, the only solution is to make sure there's no evidence of Professor Garibaldi's great historical 'find'."

"But Signor" Spalanzini spluttered, "the bronze statue of Deidamia…"

"*What* bronze statue?" Macchiato said with crooked smile. "We go with Plan B at noon tomorrow."

Plan B? What was Plan B?

He glanced my way. I tried to look as dumb as possible. "And we keep the girl, just in case. If everything goes according to plan, we claim she was simply my dinner guest. If not, she's shark food."

I tried not to show what I was feeling – which was downright terror.

Sofronia yawned and Signor Macchiato told her to can it. The dinner party was over.

That slimeball Monocolo locked me in my cabin. I can't sleep. I have to get out of here and warn Gianni and Uncle Tad that something's going on. But they don't even know where I am!

If I could give a signal!

I shivered and pulled dad's Princeton jacket around my shoulders – the Princeton jacket! I *knew* it would bring me

CHAPTER 27

luck! I slipped it off and wedged it into the porthole so that the lettering faced the shore. *Please*, let someone see it!

I must have dozed off for a minute, because a sound outside suddenly jerked me awake. I opened the porthole and stuck my head out, but it was so dark I couldn't see a thing. Then I heard a gentle splashing sound – and a very weak 'woof'!

It was Nero, looking half-drowned! He must've swum out from the shore! He was having a hard time keeping himself afloat. The surface of the water was about four feet below the porthole, so there was no way I could reach him. The Princeton jacket!

I grabbed it by the sleeves, making a kind of sling, then lowered it down for him to crawl into. It took him three attempts, he was so exhausted. Eventually I hauled him up through the porthole and wrapped him in all the towels I could find in the bathroom. He was pretty much out of it, and I was just wondering if mouth-to-mouth resuscitation worked on dogs, when he opened one eye and gave me a sort of watery smile. Then I burst into tears and made him wetter than ever.

It was several minutes before I even noticed the set of keys he'd laid at my feet – all neatly labeled – the key to my cabin and the ignition keys to the two launches!

CHAPTER 28

NERO'S MEMOIRS

Caroline opened the cabin door a crack. "Come on, Nero," she whispered. "We're out of here."

We looked into the narrow hallway and as we edged past a series of cabin doors, we heard the reassuring sound of snoring.

We were almost to the staircase at the end of the hallway, when we heard something we didn't want to hear – the squeak of a doorknob turning. We froze. We heard a whispered "Buona notte, caro". A cabin door swung open and out stepped Sofronia Macchiato!

I fully expected her to raise the alarm at once, but she didn't. She just stood and stared at us for a long time. The following conversation was confusing and I didn't get the deeper meanings, but I quote it for what It's worth.

"Caroline! I thought you'd be asleep by now."

"Likewise."

Now a tall man came out of the cabin. He wasn't wearing a shirt. Sofronia must've woken him up. Or maybe he walked in his sleep.

"This – uh – this is Fabrizio, the cook" Sofronia stammered. "I teach him English."

"At four in the morning?" Caroline asked.

"He works long hours – this is the only time we have. We are reading 'Moby Dick' together.

"'Winnie the Pooh' might be better for beginners – but then, Fabrizio doesn't look like a beginner."

I didn't get any of this. If *I* was locked up with the cook at four in the morning, I'd have been swapping recipes.

Caroline smiled. "Actually, I was just on my way to see your husband. I want to borrow the launch. I'm sure he won't mind."

"No! You cant –" Sofronia gasped. "My husband needs his sleep."

"We don't have to wake him if you don't want to. Maybe Fabrizio could show me the way."

"Si, si – but quietly!" She muttered something to the tall guy rapidly in Italian – I guess her English lessons hadn't included nautical commands. She gave Caroline a curt goodnight and made a dignified exit up the stairs.

Fabrizio the cook didn't look too thrilled about any of this. He picked me up, tossed me over his shoulder and led the way up top. The motor launch was tied up off the rear deck of the yacht. Fabrizio helped Caroline in and explained the controls to her.

"Sure you know how to operate a launch?" he asked.

"I'm a sailor from way back," she said. "Just call me Ishmael."

She turned the key and the motor started up. It sounded deafening in the still night air. Fabrizio leant down to hand me to Caroline and she reached up for me.

"Grazie tante, Fabrizio," she said, "e buona fortuna con le lezioni di Inglese"

"Your Italian is very good, Signorina. Let me congratulate you."

It was Macchiato. He'd appeared out of nowhere, an evil-smelling cigar stuffed in his mouth. He grabbed me by the scruff of my neck – I *hate* that – then with his free hand, he slugged Fabrizio so hard he went sprawling across the deck.

"No doubt you understood everything my guests discussed over dinner?"

"Every word" Caroline said.

"Get out of the launch."

"Give me the dog."

"Get out of the launch!"

"*Give me the dog!*"

Signor Macchiato held me higher in the air. "This dog Signorina? What a swimmer!" He held me out over the side of the boat. "Let's see him swim now."

I looked down, but wished I hadn't.

"No!" Caroline cried. She started to climb out. Signor Macchiato smiled a greasy smile and pulled me out of her reach and close to his face. This was too easy. I craned forward and sank my teeth into his nose.

He howled like a dog and dropped me onto the deck. I took a flying leap into the launch. His cigar fell from his mouth and landed in the launch right by me.

Caroline started the motor, rammed it into forward gear and we took off. The last thing I heard as we skimmed across the water was Macchiato yelling "Get me a rabies shot!"

I don't think Caroline was as good a sailor as she'd boasted. We went slow, we went fast, we weaved back and forth, and a couple of times, we bounced so hard I was nearly thrown out of the boat.

She swerved suddenly to avoid hitting a fishing boat and I was thrown to the floor. That was when I noticed a big can lying on its side. It must have been knocked over when we bounced. Liquid poured out of it – it had the same pungent stench as the stuff they put into cars and motor scooters – gasoline!

In the normal run of a dog's life, there's little chance of coming into contact with gasoline, but *this* dog's life had been far from normal for the past few weeks. What I *did* know about gasoline is that it can be dangerous if not actually *inside* a car or motor scooter. And the foul smelling stuff was inching towards Macchiato's cigar!

I barked a warning to Caroline, but she was too busy zigging and zagging to pay any attention to me. "Hold on Nero!" she yelled. To what, I thought – and *with* what? Paws don't hack it when it comes to 'holding on'.

Another big bounce, and while I was airborne, I could see the marina dead ahead – we were heading straight for the pier! I came down from the bounce and landed – not in the boat – in the water!

As I splashed down, I heard Caroline's anguished call – "*Nero!*"

I struggled to the surface and caught a glimpse of Caroline pulling on the steering wheel in an effort to get back to me. But the boat just kept going round in circles. I paddled to the pier, but it was too high for me to climb out. Then, a hand grabbed me and hauled me out of the drink.

"I've got you!"

It was Gianni – a much soberer Gianni than the one I left behind. He tucked me under his arm and darted behind a trash can as Monocolo strode to the end of the pier with a cell phone clamped to his ear.

"You want I should take care of the girl?" he laughed. "With pleasure Signor."

Gianni and I looked out to sea, and what did we see? We saw – FIRE! Macchiato's cigar had ignited the gasoline and the launch was burning! And it was coming straight at us!

It hit the pier with a splintering crash followed by a shattering explosion!

Flames billowed from the launch and lit up the night. Monocolo shielded himself against flying shards of burning timber. Gianni cried out, but Monocolo didn't hear him – he just opened his cell phone and said "The girl, she is taken care of Signor." He chuckled happily to himself as he strolled off down the pier without a backward glance.

Gianni dropped me and ran to the edge of the pier. He fell to his hands and knees shouting "Caroline! CAROLINE!" I wanted to howl, but Gianni was doing enough for both of us.

We heard a splashing sound over the crackle of the flames. A hand emerged from the water, then a head – Caroline's!

Gianni grabbed her hand and hauled her up onto the pier where she lay absolutely still.

"Caroline! Say something!"

Caroline spat water and said "I thought this kinda thing only happened to Nancy Drew."

I've never seen a guy hug a girl as tight as Gianni hugged Caroline, not even in the movies. Then they hugged me, taking the wind out of me.

We all walked cautiously back to the scooter.

"You look terrible" Caroline said.

"I have the overhang" Gianni explained.

CHAPTER 29

CAROLINE'S JOURNAL

Saturday July 30

I was wet through and the rising sun did nothing to warm me, so Nero and I shivered on the back of the scooter as Gianni sped back towards Torre del Greco. He did his usual scary thing of talking on his cell phone as we went.

"Si Professore! She is safe with me! We are going to the foundry! You must call Detective Sammartini and get a search warrant!"

"That'll take too long!" I yelled against the rush of the wind. "Macchiato's going for Plan B at noon!"

"What is this Plan B?" Gianni yelled back.

"No idea! But sure as hell he's not aiming for the Nobel Peace Prize!"

We passed a roadside billboard which Nero seemed to take an intense interest in, and he strained to look over my shoulder as we passed it. It had a picture of a dog with an inane grin and it was for some kind of dog food – 'Cane Favorito', I think. Trust Nero to be thinking of food at a time like this.

The sun was up by the time we approached the foundry. The place still looked deserted, though there was a large black car parked nearby with two men in black suits lounging against it – Macchiato's thugs. Gianni cut the engine and coasted into a parking spot near a dumpster.

As we got off the scooter, a little green van chugged towards us. We ducked behind the dumpster. Every hair on Nero's back suddenly stood on end and he growled.

"Shh!" I said and he stopped growling, but his ears were up and he watched the green van intently as – Bottiglione and his skinny sidekick Luigi got out. They sat on the sidewalk, just feet from where we were hiding.

"Fantastico!" Gianni said under his breath, slapping his forehead with his hand in a very Italian way. "Just what we need!"

Bottiglione dragged a piece of salami from under his jacket and commenced to gnaw at it. He spoke with his fat mouth full.

"Wouldn't ya know the boss would pick today to get us over here? Just when we got other fish to fry."

Luigi frowned. "We're havin' fish? It ain't Friday."

Bottiglione swiped him with the salami. "That was a rhetorical embellishment, ya dummy. By 'fish' I mean 'dogs'."

Luigi looked completely lost. "Okaaaay..."

Bottiglione produced a bottle of Chianti from somewhere on his person and took a swig. "Just think, after today, no more mangy dogs."

"What a relief" Luigi said.

"You can say that again."

"What a relief."

Bottiglione swiped him again.

CHAPTER 29

Nero wriggled out of my arms. I held my breath, thinking he'd head straight for the two clowns by the van – but he didn't. He crouched low and started up the street away from us. He took a quick look over his shoulder to make sure Bottiglione and Luigi hadn't seen him, then took off at a run.

CHAPTER 30

NERO'S MEMOIRS

The pasta factory looked as dead and dingy as before, except there was now a sleeping dog chained to the wooden security gate – Caligula.

I made a rough estimate of the length of his chain, then stationed myself a bit beyond that and sat facing him. I tried to sound as casual as possible.

"Caligula old buddy!"

He opened his eyes and fixed me with a glassy stare.

"Fancy seeing you here!" I said cheerfully. Then I noticed there were bloody streaks all over his muzzle and shoulders and I stood up in shock. Even a Doberman shouldn't have to put up with that! Maybe Caligula was ready to come back to our side. "Have those guys been beating you?"

He closed his eyes. "Leave me alone."

"I hear the butchers are coming for the dogs at noon."

No response.

"Guess you'll be out of a job. Any future plans?" Caligula either hadn't heard a word or wasn't listening. "Bottiglione won't have much use for you after today, he might as well ship you off with the others."

Still nothing. All the fight seemed to have gone out of him. Had his conscience deserted him too? "How are my pals doing inside? Mind if I say hi to them?"

He just lifted his head, turned it away from me, and settled it down on his paws again.

I walked up to the security gate and listened: not a sound. I peered through the cracks between the planks.

"Can anyone hear me?"

"Who wants to know?"

"Nero. Nero from Pompeii!"

A few voices mumbled. "Nero. Whassup Nero?" None of them sounded alarmed in any way. Then, one voice that I knew well:

"Nero!" It was Rufus. He scrambled up to the door and stuck his nose out through a crack. "Hey old buddy. How's tricks?"

"Rufus, we gotta get you out of there!"

"Why?"

I was so startled by this response, I couldn't think of what to say next.

"Sure, it's a bit cramped in here" Rufus said happily, "but those dumbos are feeding us regular as clockwork. Think you could get Drusilla and the pups down here? I hate to thinka them scroungin' for food while we're livin' the good life."

Dogs and food! Same old story! Eating has always clouded our judgment! Time was running out! I racked my brain trying to come up with something Bogie would do in a situation like this – then it hit me like a rock! Humphrey Bogart had never *been* in a situation like this! All my life I'd been barking up the wrong guy! It was all up to me! *Me*, Nero!

"Rufus, listen! Get everyone up!"

Rufus yawned. "Tough call buddy. Just had breakfast. We're all wiped out."

"Trust me! Breakfast will be your last meal unless you get everyone up NOW!"

Rufus sounded as if he had no idea where I was aiming, but he said "Hey you guys, up on your paws! Nero's got something to say."

There were a few tired murmurs of 'get outta here', 'quiet', 'siddown'.

"*Geddup!*" Rufus barked. Nothing but a few snores. "Okey dokey, while you're all settled down, nice 'n' cozy, I got a good one for ya. This poodle walks into a bar see, and the bartender says..."

There were groans and a few cries of 'oh no' and 'not again' and 'quit with the jokes' and the dogs all dragged themselves upright. Rufus stuck his nose back through the crack.

"They're all yours buddy, take it away."

"Listen up guys! We gotta make a lotta noise!"

"Like, who's got the energy to bark?" a lazy voice said. "Wake me for lunch", said another.

"*Listen!* You know why those lowlifes are feeding you? They're taking you to the dog food factory!"

"Terrific! More food!" Rufus observed.

"Yeah" I said, "and *you're it!* They're gonna mince you up and put you in cans and feed you to the dogs!"

Silence now. They were listening.

"*That's* why they've been fattening you up! Bark now guys, or you're dog food! All together, after me: *we want out!*"

A few dogs echoed the cry, but without much enthusiasm. I repeated it. "*We want out!* C'mon guys!"

Now a bunch joined in: "We want out!" And more and more dogs barked: "*We want out*! WE WANT OUT! *WE WANT OUT!*"

Caligula scrambled to his feet. "What are you doing? You'll get me in trouble!"

Over the sound of barking, there was another sound – a truck approaching. I turned to see a sleek produce truck pulling in to the parking bay. On its side was a picture of a dog with a stupid grin – the Cane Favorito Dog Food truck!

CHAPTER 31

CAROLINE'S JOURNAL

We'd been crouching behind the dumpster for so long the entire left side of my body had gone numb, and I doubted I'd ever have any feeling in it again.

Bottiglione and his skinny sidekick were still bickering and complaining and talking about dog food, of all things!

Gianni suddenly sat up straight. "That barking – is it Nero?"

"Probably. I expect he's found an ice-cream truck or something."

Bottiglione heard it too. He went to the middle of the street and looked in the direction the sound was coming from. There were other dogs barking now. Lots and lots of dogs barking up a storm.

"What the hell's goin' on up there? Go take a look" Bottiglione shouted at Luigi.

Luigi sat where he was. "Not me, I've had it with those mutts."

Macchiato's two henchmen strolled over from the big black car. "Hey, you two! Keep those dogs quiet! The boss'll be here any minute!"

Luigi dragged himself to his feet and he and Bottiglione hurried up the street. The two henchmen followed a short way.

Gianni jumped up. "Now's our chance!"

We ran across the street and slipped in through the foundry door. Now, in broad daylight, we saw what we hadn't seen last night: the foundry was vast. The roof, criss-crossed with girders and cables and pulleys, was a good hundred and twenty feet above us.

There was a roaring sound and waves of heat rolled over us. In the center of the space was a gigantic furnace. The place was crawling with men in heatproof suits and hard hats – none of them had noticed us yet.

Gianni looked up and clutched my arm. I followed his horrified gaze. Suspended above the furnace was the bronze statue of Deidamia!

"What are they going to do?" I whispered.

He could hardly speak from emotion. "I think they plan to melt her down" he said. "Don't you see? It's perfect – if they sank her to the bottom of the sea, or buried her, or even broke her up, there's still a chance someone might find the evidence. This way she'll disappear without a trace and no one will ever know."

I looked up at the beautiful Deidamia, over two thousand years old, Uncle Tad's pride and joy, the culmination of all his hard work. "There must be something we can do!"

Gianni looked up at the network of catwalks mounting almost to the roof of the space. "If we could just get up there..."

"How are we going to do that? One of those guys will stop us."

"Not if we're in disguise." He pointed. To our left, hanging neatly on pegs, were rows of overalls and hard hats and protective gloves.

CHAPTER 31

The gloves made my hands look like I was from outer space and I had to roll up the legs of the pants so I could walk without falling over myself. But no one took any notice of us as we moved cautiously across the foundry floor.

There was a rusty spiral staircase on the back wall that wound all the way up to the roof. Gianni led the way and we climbed – and climbed – and climbed.

I looked down and wished I hadn't. "Is this a good time to tell you I'm scared of heights?" Gianni just sighed.

"Come una bambina!" he said. It sounded like a compliment, until I realized he meant 'don't be such a girl.'

At last we reached a catwalk about sixty or seventy feet above the floor. We were dead level with Deidamia.

"You see those steel cables holding the statue?" Gianni said. "They go up through a pulley system to the roof, then across the roof and down the far wall to a counterweight over there."

He pointed to a sort of vertical railroad mounted on the far wall. It ran all the way up to the roof and, halfway down, level with the suspended statue, was the counterweight – a stack of grimy lead weights about ten feet long.

"It works like an elevator. The counterweight is perfectly balanced so that the statue can be lowered into the furnace at the pull of a cable – simple physics."

I was wished I'd paid more attention in science class. Who'd have thought that stuff would ever come in handy?

"You mean it only takes one person to lower the statue?" I said.

"Exactly." Gianni pointed to a guy way below us on the floor, his hand poised above a red lever. The words on his overall read 'Caporeparto'. I guessed he was the foreman.

"If he's down there, why are we all the way up here?"

"Because if I can get onto the counterweight, my weight will throw the balance and stop them lowering the statue into the furnace."

My jaw dropped open. "Then what?"

"I hang on until the professor arrives with the police. Simple."

"That might be hours!"

"You have a better idea?"

"But these guys are animals, and…" I didn't finish the sentence, but in my mind it went something like "…and I don't want anything to happen to you." But I clammed up. I didn't want him to think I was even more of a girl than he already did.

I looked at the counterweight mounted on the tracks on the far wall. "How do we even get to the counterweight from here?"

He pointed up. Another fifty feet above us, just under the roof, was an even higher catwalk. This was all getting way too scary and it was unbearably hot. I wiped sweat out of my eyes as we continued up the rusted stairs, higher and higher, until we were right under the roof. The floor was a long, long way down.

Gianni helped me onto the catwalk – he had to, my eyes were closed.

CHAPTER 31

We started across. My foot slipped a few times, but Gianni steadied me each time. About half way there, we were directly above the furnace and felt the searing updraft of heat from its flames.

When we were close to the other side, there was a commotion below. We glanced down to see Macchiato and Sofronia being greeted like visiting royalty. He was in his immaculate cream suit with the usual cigar stuck in his face. He also had a big sticking plaster over his nose. *Score one for Nero.* And Sofronia had really outdone herself – she was wearing a minuscule white silk dress – I would've described it as virginal white, but somehow the description didn't quite fit. Her heels were higher than ever and her neckline lower than ever and, yeah, she was wearing more jewelry than they have in Tiffany's window at Christmas.

"Hurry!" Gianni guided me across the catwalk.

We reached the other side as Macchiato and Sofronia were seated in grand style right in front of the furnace. Clearly, he wanted a ringside seat at Deidamia's execution.

Gianni clamped his gloves around the greasy steel cables holding the counterweight and stepped off the catwalk. I held my breath as he slid downward, streaking his overall with black grease.

Just as his feet touched the top of the lead weights, there were three sharp, piercing blasts of a siren which startled him and he nearly lost his balance.

Below, Macchiato gave the foreman a nod and he pushed the red lever down. There was a grinding of gears and the counterweight started upward – and Deidamia started down towards the flames!

Gianni bounced his weight up and down on the counterweight and with a screech of metal on metal, the whole mechanism shuddered to a halt.

Gianni looked up at me with a wide grin and gave me a thumbs up.

They weren't so happy down below. The foreman pushed and pulled at the lever, but nothing happened.

Macchiato was furious. "Get it moving!"

A few other overalled guys joined in and they tweaked some cables. The foreman threw the lever again and – the statue shuddered and started to descend again – and the counterweight moved upward with Gianni perched unsteadily on top. He shot a desperate glance up to me – he wasn't heavy enough!

Time to stop being a girl. I closed my eyes and did as I'd seen Gianni do – I clamped my gloved hands around the greasy cable. Immediately, I slipped about twenty feet. I heard Gianni gasp and I opened one eye to see him reaching up to me. To do what? Catch me if I fell? Fat chance. There was nothing between me and the concrete floor a hundred feet below. Gianni's hands found my ankles and he eased me onto the counterweight next to him.

My added weight took effect immediately. With a loud *crunch*, the pulley system ground to a halt again. Below us, Deidamia came to a stop, swaying gently about six feet above the flames. Somewhere in the back of my mind, which was racing now, I thought *what does this remind me of?* Of course! Vesuvius! Flames pouring out of the crater – the treasures of Pompeii about to be consumed!

CHAPTER 31

A red light flashed somewhere above our heads and a siren blared. "What's going on up there?" Macchiato yelled.

"Just a temporary hitch, Signor," the foreman said. "This equipment is very old."

"I don't have time for temporary hitches!" Macchiato fumed. "I want this business over as quickly as possible!"

A jolt on the counterweight nearly toppled us from it. A loud grinding sound echoed round the foundry as the counterweight started upward again.

Gianni said in an anguished whisper, "We're *still* not heavy enough!" We kept rising. We were almost to the roof now and Deidamia was closer than ever to the flames. Gianni fumbled desperately in the pockets of his overall and found a wrench. He jammed it into the counterweight rail tracks. There was a *screech* and the counterweight stopped its ascent. I glanced down and saw that Deidamia had stopped just a few feet from the mouth of the furnace.

Below, Macchiato's fury erupted in a stream of Italian expletives that I'd never learnt at home.

Gianni beamed a smile at me and raised his fist in a power salute. Wrong move. A hand grabbed his upheld wrist and hauled him bodily off the top of the counterweight. His feet dangled over – nothing! We looked up into the single, cold, glaring eye of Monocolo.

"I think I found the hitch Signor."

CHAPTER 32

NERO'S MEMOIRS

The barking was deafening now.

The driver got out of the Cane Favorito truck and scratched his head. Bottiglione and Luigi ran in from the street, their faces flushed.

"What's going on?" the driver asked.

Bottiglione had no idea. He wiped sweat off his face. "We gotta get 'em to the butcher *now!* If Signor Macchiato finds out we been workin' this little swindle…" Then he caught sight of me. "*You!*" He turned to Caligula. "*Go get him!*"?

Caligula didn't move.

"*Ya hear me?*" Bottiglione yelled. Caligula remained motionless. Bottiglione grabbed a hefty stick from the ground and started beating him. Caligula cowered. Enough! No dog, not even Caligula deserved to be treated that way. I launched myself at Bottiglione. He saw me coming and sidestepped and, as he swiped at me with the stick, I caught it in my jaws and hung on.

He raised the stick until I was hanging level with his bloodshot eyes. He shot a sidelong glance at the stone wall and I knew what was coming – he was going to slam me against it!

Suddenly, Caligula stirred. He stood up, bared his teeth and advanced on Bottiglione. Bottiglione's laugh died and he backed up, farther and farther until Caligula reached the limit of his chain. Bottiglione sneered at him. "Whatcha gonna do now, ya dumb canine?"

I let go of the stick and dropped to the ground.

"*PULL!*" I barked at Caligula. Then I turned to the rickety wooden door to my pals' prison. "*PUSH!*"

They all got the message. Caligula strained on his chain – the imprisoned dogs rushed the door. It splintered and came off its hinges.

Dogs, hundreds of dogs spilled out, tumbling over one another in their eagerness to get at Bottiglione. He backed up to a wall searching frantically for escape, but the dogs were all over him in a flash. He toppled to the ground. Dogs nipped at his clothes, his fingers, his feet until he was trapped under a blanket of seething fur.

The Cane Favorito guy turned tail and ran. He jumped into his truck, backed out of the loading bay and sped off kicking up dust.

Bottiglione freed a hand from the mountain of dogs and raised it towards Luigi. "Get me outta here!" Luigi stood stock still. "*Ya hear me ya dummy?*"

Luigi stood indignantly erect and said quietly "Dummy yourself." Then he went to Caligula and released him from his chain.

Caligula walked slowly to where Bottiglione lay. All the dogs sensed his menace and cleared a path. But Caligula didn't so much as utter a snarl. He just padded up to the quaking Bottiglione and took a long look at him. Then he raised his hind leg and peed on him.

All the dogs yipped and yelped in sheer joy. Rufus rolled on the ground laughing. Having done, Caligula turned his back to Bottiglione and with his hind legs, kicked dirt onto him. Then he sauntered off up the street.

Bottiglione made a move to rise, but the dogs snarled and he stayed put. I needed a platform – a soapbox; in the absence of one, I climbed onto Bottiglione's belly. There were howls and barks of "Nero! Nero!"

Everywhere I looked I saw friendly faces: Drusus, Tiberius, Florian, Julius, Mira, one-eyed Cato, Castor and Pollux, Lepidus, Octavius, Marcus, Antonius, Brutus, Cassius, Casca, Trebonius, Ligarius, Antonia and her pups, Claudius, Germanicus, Cicero, Portia, Calpurnia, Volumnia, Coriolanus... more than I could name, all barking, 'NERO, NERO, NERO!' I never knew that I had so many friends.

I raised a paw to quiet them. "Fellow canines! Dogs of Pompeii!" They quietened. "Our human friends are in danger!"

"So what?" a dog said.

"It's the humans who wanted to kill us all" another growled.

I waited until the naysayers were done, then I continued the way some guy called Marlon Brandy did in a great movie about ancient Rome, 'Julius Caesar'. Okay, he was no Bogart, but he could sure work a crowd.

'We must not condemn an entire species for the acts of a few lowdown dirty crooks! Since the dawn of civilization, man has been our ally! No dog is alone when man is his companion – and no man is alone who has a dog by his side!"

There were a few murmurs of 'true' and 'you said it'.

"Honor our noble alliance! Fight for *our* freedom – and *theirs!* And this day will go down in dog history!

The dogs growled amongst themselves. I was winning them over.

"Remember our proud heritage! Remember the vow of our ancestors – 'To those who would harm us, our home or our loved ones – *beware of the dog!* CAVE CANEM!"

As one, the dogs cried "CAVE CANEM!"

I jumped down from Bottiglione and ran for the street. The dogs followed chanting "CAVE CANEM! CAVE CANEM! CAVE CANEM!"

CHAPTER 33

CAROLINE'S JOURNAL

The only sound in the foundry was the roar of the furnace. All eyes were on us. Gianni swayed gently over the abyss. The only thing preventing him from plummeting to the floor below was Monocolo's vise like grip on his wrist.

"Try it now!" Monocolo called to the foreman.

The foreman heaved at the lever. Nothing moved.

Monocolo fixed his attention on Gianni. "What did you do to it?"

Gianni was silent.

"What – did – you – do?" Monocolo asked quietly. He shifted his gaze to me and stupidly, I glanced at the wrench. Monocolo smiled.

"A wrench in the works. Not very original. Give it to me."

"*Don't do it!*" Gianni shouted.

Monocolo kept smiling. "Your friend is getting very heavy Signorina." He loosened his grip and Gianni slipped a few inches. I cried out in terror. Tears were streaming down my face now, and I could hardly see.

"Don't let him fall!" I begged Monocolo. "I'll give it to you."

"*No!*" Gianni yelled.

I eased the wrench out of the rail. There was a grinding of metal and the counterweight started slowly upward.

Monocolo reached down with his free hand. "Give me the wrench!"

"Help Gianni first! Then I'll give it to you!" I said.

With little apparent effort, Monocolo hauled Gianni up and dropped him onto the catwalk. Then he leaned over, his hand held out.

"*Give me the wrench! Now!*"

I raised it above my head and – cracked him over the skull with it. He went down onto the catwalk like a sack of potatoes.

Gianni scrambled to his feet and jumped onto the counterweight with me. "Brava!" he said and held out his hand for the wrench.

I held it out to him, but my hand shook and I dropped it. Then I did the dumbest thing I've ever done in my whole life – I reached out after it – and slipped.

Gianni cried out and grabbed for me, but missed. I grabbed for the counterweight, but it was covered in grease and I couldn't get a grip. I slid to the bottom edge where there was a ridge just wide enough to hook my fingers onto. It all happened so quickly. I hung there swaying, and heard the *clang* as the wrench hit the concrete far below.

My heart was thumping so loudly, I thought it would burst through my ribcage.

Sofronia was the first to give voice to any concern those below might have had. "*Do something!*" she screamed.

The foreman ran to the lever and stopped the machinery.

"Start it again" Macchiato said.

"Signor Macchiato..."

CHAPTER 33

"*Start the mechanism!*"

No one moved a hair. Macchiato flung his cigar to the ground and pushed the foreman aside. He grabbed the lever with both hands… and then we heard barking. Lots and lots and *lots* of barking.

Hundreds of dogs bounded into the foundry. Chairs went flying, workers were toppled, Sofronia went down like a ninepin. But the dogs knew their target and went straight for Macchiato.

Sirens pierced the air and outside, police cars screeched to a halt.

"Hold on" Gianni said. I risked an upward glance and saw him tearing off his gloves. "Give me your hand!"

I reached up with my gloved hand. He grabbed it and my oversize glove slid off. I nearly lost my hold on the ridge. Gianni reached again.

"*Give me your hand!*"

"I can't!"

"*Yes you can!*"

I couldn't move.

"You American girls!" Gianni said. "You are all – how do you say – pappamolle!"

"Pappamolle?" I said stupidly.

"Wimps!" he yelled.

Wimps! That did it. I reached up until his fingers touched mine. His hand wound round my wrist and, slowly but surely, he pulled me up onto the counterweight.

I should've said thank you, but all that came out was

"*Wimps?*"

"Except you" Gianni said tenderly. "You are the bravest girl I know." And he put his arms around me and held me tight.

Below us, two bloodied hands emerged from the mountain of savage, barking dogs, then a couple of shredded cream linen sleeves. Detective Sammartini clamped handcuffs onto the wrists.

"Giorgio Macchiato, I am arresting you for theft, conspiracy to destroy Italian government property, kidnapping, endangering the life of an American citizen –" He went on and on.

Sofronia fainted. Another little white dress bit the dust.

Uncle Tad and Fiona appeared. "Caroline!" Uncle Tad called, searching the jumble of bodies for me. Then Fiona looked up, saw us and screamed.

Gianni and I paid no attention. His lips were centimeters from mine and I sure wasn't going to stop him – then there was a jolt and the counterweight started to rise again. Gianni lost interest in me at once. "We need another twenty pounds!"

There was a familiar bark and we turned to see Nero clambering across the catwalk towards us.

"How heavy would you say Nero is?" Gianni asked.

"Oh, about twenty... NO!"

"Nero!" he called.

"Nero, don't do it!"

But Nero seemed to be calculating the distance between himself and us. He crouched, then sprang. He arced gracefully through the air and landed in Gianni's arms.

CHAPTER 33

The machinery stopped.

We looked down at Deidamia, swaying inches above the flames. She'd survived Vesuvius, she'd survived burial for two thousand years, and she'd survived Macchiato too.

CHAPTER 34

NERO'S MEMOIRS

Next morning Rufus and I set out bright and early. It was a beautiful, clear day. As we trotted out through Porta di Sarno and past the villa site, work was already starting up again and the Professor was giving instructions to all the students. I wondered whether one of them would find my tennis ball. Then I told myself forget it. Sometimes you just have to let go of stuff.

Keeping Vesuvius ahead of us as a guide, we walked north-west. The road started to climb as we reached the lower slopes of the volcano and soon we were walking between vineyards. We walked on through the night barely feeling tired, and as the sun rose the next morning, we were on the track leading up to the abandoned barn.

"Nero!" It was Olivia! She raced out of the barn and down the hill to meet us. "I knew you'd come back!"

Drusilla put her head out of the barn and gave a happy yelp. Five small heads popped out beside her and Rufus barked joyously and ran to them. The pups jumped all over him, knocking him to the ground and they all rolled around barking and yipping.

I told Olivia and Drusilla everything that had happened – in a nutshell. Rufus joined in, somewhat exaggerating his part in it all. Drusilla wouldn't give him an even break though.

"Don't you *ever* get yourself into trouble like that again, you hear? What kind of example are you setting for the pups?"

Olivia never took her eyes off mine. "Oh Nero, I'm so proud of you" she sighed.

"Don't give him a swelled head Olivia." Augustus lumbered over to us. "He was merely doing his duty as a Dog of Pompeii."

"Gee, thanks Augustus" I said – like, don't lavish me with *too* much praise. Then I heard a voice that was familiar, but unexpected.

"Hey dude! How's tricks?"

"Samson!"

"Samson's been very helpful" Olivia said. "He brought food and..."

"Aaah, it was nuttin" Samson said modestly. "I figured it was time to see the world. Didn't wanna wake up one day and find I'd never been further than the end of my chain. And, uh..." he gave Olivia a shy grin, "your pals were pretty persuasive."

Olivia lowered her eyes. I looked from one to the other and got the picture. I should've been happy for them, but somehow, I just felt kind of empty inside.

*

There was a big celebration when we got home. Umberto's was jumping and there were more dogs than humans!

Tony, Vittorio and Fiammetta were kept on their toes feeding us all. Even Umberto made a special effort to

CHAPTER 34

be nice to us dogs. *Make the most of it guys*, I thought, *it won't last.*

Everyone made speeches – except the dogs, of course.

Detective Sammartini gave us the lowdown on Macchiato. Seems he'd committed about twenty-five different crimes against the state, the city of Pompeii, the port of Naples, even United Nations. Apparently Pompeii was declared a World Heritage site in 1997, a fact that Macchiato and his legal eagles had overlooked. Macchiato was heading for the slammer and he wouldn't be out anytime soon.

Bottiglione and Luigi were carted off to jail with the rest of Signor Macchiato's guys, and best of all, a severely concussed Monocolo was resting not-so-comfortably in the prison hospital. Yay Caroline!

The Pompeii special commissioner was the guest of honor. "From now on" he said, "the dogs of Pompeii will be granted their own identity and dignity; their health and well-being will be a prime issue and an adoption program will be organized." Maybe the pups will have a happy future after all.

Caroline made a short speech and said this was the best vacation she'd ever had and, oh yeah, she mentioned that I was the bravest dog she'd ever met. Shucks.

Gianni took the floor and talked about the special relationship between 'homo sapiens and canis familiaris' – that's 'man and dog' to you and me. He said this alliance had endured for fifteen thousand years. His speech was nearly as long. But the kid had come a long way for someone who used to call me 'the dog.'

Finally, the Professor stood up and all the students cheered him. He's worth quoting:

"To an archaeologist, his job is his home. And that job takes him wherever the myths and legends of the ancient world might be uncovered. But in all my years of traveling around the world, searching for the treasures of the past, perhaps I failed to see the most important treasures of all – those that dwell in my heart – the treasures of family..." he took Caroline's hand and she smiled, "...and loyal friends." He put a hand on Fiona's shoulder and she burst into *tears!* Humans are hard to figure. Whatever happened to *laughing* when you're happy?

Later, when most of the party had gone and the waiters were clearing tables, Caroline and Gianni were still talking.

"Next week I go back to school in Naples" Gianni was saying, "but I come back here to help the Professor when he needs me. And you?"

"I'm going to apply for the American School in Rome." Caroline said.

"Rome!"

"Sure! They do a neat course in ancient history."

"Is very close, Rome" Gianni said, and he took her hand.

I guess those two kids are really stuck on each other.

Yep, the world was doing okay. So why did I feel so down? Maybe it was because someone was missing from the party – someone who's part Greyhound on her father's side.

A dog wandered by and nodded to me. "Hand it to ya Nero, ya did well."

"Thanks Julius."

"It's Claudius."

He didn't seem to mind I got his name wrong.

"First rule of leadership Nero! Remember the names of every dog in your pack!" Augustus got up from under a table where he'd been watching me.

"We can't all be perfect Augustus."

"No, but leaders must *aspire* to perfection. Remember that my boy. Because one day... one day..." And he wandered off into the night.

I didn't have the heart to tell the old guy I had other plans.

CHAPTER 35

CAROLINE'S JOURNAL

Monday, 1st August

The vet gave Nero a clean bill of health and all the necessary shots and documents for bringing him into the States.

Dad was fine about the idea of another dog in the family, but Mom quibbled a bit. She kept asking things like, 'is he house-trained?' and 'will we all have to learn Italian commands?' He's certainly house-trained – hotel-trained, even – and as far as I can tell he understands just as much English as Italian. What bothers me is the fact he's really a street dog. Even though we've got a big backyard, will it be enough?

*

American Airlines Flight 109

Naples, Capodichino – New York, JFK

Tuesday August 2

I can hardly believe it's all over. I have so much to tell them back home, but how much of it will they actually believe? Already I can see Didi rolling her eyes and saying 'puh-leeze!' at everything I say, and all she'll really want to know is about Gianni.

Maybe I should just erase a few entries out of my iPad journal and keep my mouth zipped. Too much info might not sit well with the folks – last thing I want is to be grounded. And the more I tell Didi about Gianni, the more she'll want to hear, and I think I want to keep him all to myself.

The party at Umberto's was a blast! Everyone was there and they all made speeches. Fiona actually looked quite attractive. I spent an hour helping with her makeup and hair – it looked really great once we ditched the hairpins and let it curl down to her shoulders. She was kinda blind without her glasses, but I did the mascara myself. I hope Uncle Tad noticed.

When they saw me off at the airport, Uncle Tad presented me with a first edition of The Greek Myths. He wrote a dedication to me in the front comparing me to Penthesilea (looked her up – she was Queen of the Amazons and greatly distinguished herself in battle. Cool!)

Now comes the sad part.

I'd got Nero's travel plans together. Uncle Tad helped organize the flight details and Gianni and I drove into Naples to buy him a special traveling cage. (They said he'd have to travel in the hold.)

He'd been staying at the hotel with me since he got his shots and everything, but he'd been moping a lot. Something was making him unhappy and even Fiammetta's Bistecca alla Diavola only got a token tailwag from him. He didn't seem to want to visit his friends in Pompeii; I guess that's what convinced me he'd be happier with me in the States.

Anyhow, last night, after the farewell dinner, I took him out for his last walk-of-the-day. We didn't use the leash; he was over that. He stayed by my side until, up ahead, one of his pals from the city appeared – a pretty fierce looking Pit Bull. Nero hung back a while, but the Pit Bull seemed friendly enough. He wagged his tail a lot and sat down by Nero. So I left them to it and walked on up the street. When I turned back, Nero was alone. I called him, but he didn't seem to hear me. So I went up to him and said, "Come on, time for bed."

I reached out to stroke his head and he backed away. I reached out again and again he backed away. He seemed conflicted. He took a glance over his shoulder towards Pompeii, then turned those big brown eyes back to me.

And I understood.

He didn't once take his eyes from mine as I unfastened the collar round his neck. When I'd finished, he gave my hand a short, affectionate lick, looked at me a little longer, then turned and walked slowly towards the ruined city.

He didn't look back. If he had, he would've seen me crying.

CHAPTER 36

NERO'S MEMOIRS

The last few days before Caroline left for her home were tough. I spent those days in her hotel room mostly lying on my left side – my right was still tender from the needles stuck into it by the guy in the white coat. Caroline kept telling me it was all for the best, and what a healthy dog I'd be when we got to New Jersey.

I stayed out of Pompeii. The dogs were settling back in again and they didn't need me to figure out where their next meal was coming from.

A new life, that's what I wanted. Or was it? Up to now, I'd known only the streets of Pompeii. Maybe I wasn't cut out to be a pet.

That final night, after the bash at Umberto's, Caroline and I went out walking. I stopped in my tracks when I saw Samson. Caroline guessed we wanted to talk, so she left us to it.

He sat down beside me. "Hey dude. Hear you're leavin' town."

"Yeah, tomorrow" I said.

"There's something you oughta know before you go."

"About you and Olivia?"

"She's somethin', ain't she? I fell for that dog the minute I saw her. I did every trick I knew – sat, rolled over, begged, walked on my hind legs. Sure, she was amused, but..." A hint of sadness crept into those usually fierce eyes. "Well, if ya ain't figured it out by now, you are one dumb animal."

He stood and shook himself.

"Hey! Pompeii's no place for a dog like me! Scrounging, begging! I'm used to a life of luxury!" He gave me a grin, then he turned towards Vesuvius and sauntered off. His voice drifted back to me on the evening breeze. "Take it easy dude. And may all your troubles be little ones."

I was still standing there, thinking about what he'd said when Caroline came back. She called out to me.

"Come on, time for bed."

She reached out to stroke my head and I backed away. She looked puzzled. The last thing I wanted to do was hurt Caroline. She reached out again. I backed away. Words might've helped, but even if I could've said anything, the lump in my throat would have got in the way. I could tell from her eyes that she understood. She unfastened my collar gently.

I gave her hand a farewell lick, then turned and headed for Pompeii, my home.

The Forum was silent and deserted, not a dog to be seen. I walked down Via dell'Abondanza past the Stabian Baths and the House of Julia Felix to the Grand Palaestra. The grass of the great arena was bright in the night light. And there, beautiful in the moonlight, and still as a statue, sat Olivia.

EPILOGUE

NERO'S MEMOIRS

Villa Deidamia was pronounced the most important archaeological discovery at Pompeii in over a hundred years and the professor was given government funding to continue his work on the site. I run into him now and then down at Umberto's. Gianni calls by some weekends and comes to see me. Poor kid, he still pines for Caroline.

As for the dogs, Rufus is very much the family man now, but still likes to laugh more than any dog I know. Old Agrippina is still around, crazy as ever, and complaining that life was so much better when Macchiato was running things and her boy was his right-hand dog. Speaking of Caligula, It's rumored that the day he vanished from the pasta factory, he stowed away on a pig-iron boat to Argentina and made a fresh start there as a cattle dog. Good luck to him if it's true.

Umberto's hasn't changed much, Tony and Vittorio are still waiting tables, and Signor Umberto is as bad-tempered as ever. Fiammetta retired, and spends all day watching old movies. There's a new cook – Fabrizio. Sometimes after dinner I hear him and his wife Sofronia reading 'Moby Dick' aloud to each other in the kitchen.

But I'm not the fixture at Umberto's that I used to be. My favorite way to spend an evening these days is to sit in the Grand Palaestra and watch Olivia play with our three pups in the last light of the day. Maybe I'm finally settling down.

*

And that's the end of the story.

At least I thought it was until a week ago. Then everything changed for me again. I was giving my eldest his first lesson in public relations.

"Okay, when they say sit, you sit. They love that. Makes them think they're in control. No, don't roll over, *sit!* Watch me."

Olivia came up with our other two. "Isn't he a little young for that, darling?" she said.

"Never too soon to start, and one of these days he'll have to take over from the old man."

"But not yet" she laughed. "Here's Augustus. It's time for their history lesson."

Augustus had become very frail in recent months. He shambled up and flopped down on the grass.

"Hot," he murmured.

"You look tired" Olivia said. "Why not skip the lesson for today?"

"No, no," he said, "the young ones have to learn their heritage, same as you did, and the sooner the better, times being as they are." He smiled kindly down at the pups. "Come along, Gianni, Caroline, Vespa. Let's see what you remember from yesterday." Then he added under his breath, "The *names* they give children nowadays!"

I yawned and stretched and got comfortable so I could sit in on the lesson – it really was quite enjoyable when you knew you wouldn't have to answer questions afterwards. Augustus's voice rumbled with emotion.

"..." No birds sang and the wells and the fountains ran dry..."

Given the hazards I'd faced since the day Caroline came into my life, I realized I'd spent too much of my youth watching movies, and not enough learning about the realities of life. Don't get me wrong, both are valuable, but there must be a balance.

The familiarity of Augustus's words filled me with security – a calm assurance of who I was and who we dogs were.

"Unable to wait any longer, the dogs followed the Leader out of the city. They passed a magnificent Villa where stood the beautiful statue of Deidamia..."

I must have dozed, because the next words I heard were, "Dad, come quick!"

Augustus was lying on his side, breathing fitfully.

"Get your mother!" I said. But Olivia was already racing up to us.

"Help me up" Augustus whispered through clenched teeth. But we all stood there like idiots. "Help me up!" he said again.

Olivia and I flanked him as he struggled to his feet and limped towards the colonnade. Once there he lay down exhausted in a shady corner and Olivia gently nudged him into a more comfortable position.

The word got out and the dogs started to gather silently in the Palaestra. Soon there were dozens of them. Rufus and Drusilla came into the colonnade to be near us, but the others kept a respectful distance. Occasionally Augustus muttered something under his breath and Olivia or Drusilla bent forward to listen. Once he raised his head and said, "I have to go to the Stabian Baths. There's a tour bus coming in."

Drusilla said, "Rest, Augustus. There'll be another bus tomorrow."

We sat there until long after sunset, Olivia's head resting on my shoulder, not a sound to be heard except Augustus's labored breathing. I looked out into the dark where the Dogs of Pompeii sat still and quiet.

About midnight the very city itself seemed to hold its breath and there was a silence such as I've never heard. It was broken by a howl from Rufus that echoed round and round the ancient arena. Dog upon dog took up the cry, until the night air was filled with the sound, and I knew that my old friend was gone forever.

I sat with him all night, long after the other dogs had gone. I must have dozed towards dawn. I was woken by the sound of sobbing. It was the old guide, Giuseppe, kneeling by Augustus's side.

One evening soon after that, a deputation of dogs came to me and formally offered me the position of Leader of the Pack. I thanked them kindly, but said that it was out of the question.

That night Rufus and Drusilla came over to visit. They seemed to have rehearsed in advance, and as one, they asked me to reconsider the idea of becoming Leader.

"Me? Follow Augustus?" I said. "I don't even have the right name for it. Leaders of The Pack are always called Claudius or Marcus Aurelius, or Hadrian, or Octavius or –"

"Augustus" Olivia said.

"Exactly." I nodded. "Whoever heard of a Leader of the Pack called Nero?"

Olivia, Rufus and Drusilla exchanged a glance. "Fact is..." Rufus said haltingly, "your name *is* Augustus. Nero Augustus. Not that it matters buddy – you'd be my vote for Leader of the Pack even if your name was Bozo."

"What do you mean, 'Nero Augustus'?"

"Gus, I mean old Augustus, made me promise I'd never tell until – "He clammed up and looked to Olivia and Drusilla for support.

Drusilla was the first to speak. "Look at your right paw, Nero."

"The white one? So? Lots of dogs have one white paw. Augustus's right paw was –" And the truth began to filter through.

Finally, Olivia said "Augustus was your father, Nero. Your mother died when you were born. Augustus was heartbroken and could never bear to mention her name again. He said he didn't know how to be a father – it was better if he just watched over you from afar. That's why he left you on Signor Umberto's doorstep. But he was always there for you – if only in the background."

I thought back. Augustus always *had* been there for me, guiding, teaching, reprimanding me when I was on the wrong track. So I'd had a family after all! I'd *always* had a family, and now – I looked at Olivia and our sleeping pups – now I always would.

"Rufus is right, you know," Olivia said. "It doesn't matter what your name is. You saved Deidamia, you saved the Dogs, you saved Pompeii. You *are* the Leader of the Pack."

So now it's official. I'm Nero Augustus, Leader of the Pack, family man and respected member of society.

Sometimes I wish Caroline was around to see how much I've matured, but things are probably best the way they are. I think of her often. And sometimes when the wind is in the west and it carries the scent of Fabrizio's Cannelloni alla Marinara on the air, I say to myself, we'll always have Pompeii.

* * *

GLOSSARY OF ITALIAN
PRONUNCIATION OF NAMES

Agrippina	ah-gree-**pee**-nah
Bottiglione	bot-teel-**yoh**-nay
Caligula	kah-**leeg**-yoo-lah
Capri	**kah**-pree
Fabrizio	fah-**bree**-tsyoh
Fiammetta	fee-ahm-**met**-tah
Gianni	**jah**-nee
Giuseppe	joo-**sep**-pay
Luigi	loo-**eej**-ee
Macchiato	mac-**yah**-toh
Monocolo	mon-**ok**-ol-oh
Palaestra	pah-lay-**est**-rah
Pompeii	pom-**pay**-ee
Ravello	rah-**vel**-loh
Sammartini	sah-mar-**tee**-nee
Signora Zingarelli	seen-**yor**-ah tseen-gar-**el**-lee
Signor Umberto	seen-**yor** oom-**ber**-toh
Sofronia	so-**fron**-ya
Spalanzini	spah-lahn-**tsee**-nee

Taddeo Garibaldi	tah-**day**-oh gah-ri-**bahl**-dee
Via dell'Abbondanza	**vee**-ah del ah-bon-**dahn**-tsa
Villa Deidamia	**vee**-lah day-ee-**dah**-mya
Vittorio	vee-**tor**-yoh

WORDS AND PHRASES

amico
ah-**mee**-koh
friend

assolutamente
ahs-soh-loo-tah-**men**-tay
absolutely

Bistecca alla Diavola
bees-**tay**-kah **ahl**-lah dee-**ah**-voh-lah
steak with hot sauce

bologna
bol-**oh**-nyah
sausage made of beef, veal and pork

buon appetito
bwohn ah-peh-**tee**-toh
enjoy your food (literally: good appetite)

buon giorno
bwohn **jor**-noh
good day

buona notte, caro
bwohn-ah **not**-tay, **kah**-roh
goodnight, dear

cannelloni marinara
kahn-nel-**loh**-nee mah-ree-**nah**-rah
pasta rolls stuffed with minced meat with tomato sauce

Caffè latte per favore, e una frittata al formaggio
kah-**fay lah**-tay per fah-**vor**-ay, ay **oon**-ah free-**tah**-tah ahl for-**maj**-yoh
White coffee please, and a cheese omelet

Cane Favorito
kah-nay fah-voh-**ree**-toh
Favorite Dog

cani non ammessi
kah-nee non ahm-**may**-see
no dogs allowed

cane stupido
kah-nay **stoo**-pee-doh
stupid dog

caporeparto
kah-poh-ray-**par**-toh
foreman

Casa del Gatto
kah-sah del **gah**-toh
House of The Cat

<u>*CAVE CANEM*</u> (Latin)
kah-vay **kah**-nem
BEWARE OF THE DOG

Chinotto
kee-**not**-toh
Italian cola

ciao amico
chow ah-**mee**-koh
hello friend

Corriere della Sera
koh-ree-**er**-ay **day**-lah **say**-rah
Evening Courier (Italian newspaper)

Dio mio!
dee-oh **mee**-oh
my God!

Diversione
dee-vers-**yoh**-nay
diversion

e buona fortuna con le lezioni di Inglese
ay **bwohn**-ah for-**too**-nah kon lay lay-tsee-**oh**-nee dee een-**glay**-say
and good luck with your English lessons

grazie tante
grah-tsyay **tahn**-tay
thank you very much

merda
mer-dah
shit

muoviti il culo
mwoh-**vee**-tee eel **kool**-oh
move your ass

mi dispiace
mee dees-pee-**ah**-chay
I'm sorry

Nipote
nee-**poh**-tay
niece

non capisco
non kahp-**ees**-koh
I don't understand

Palaestra
pah-lay-**est**-rah
exercise yard

pensione
payn-see-**oh**-nay
small hotel

perché hai passi il cane?
per-**kay aa**-ee **pah**-see eel **kah**-nay
why did you throw your dog?

porta
por-tah
door or gate

Professore
proh-fes-**sor**-ay
Professor

quest'è la ragazza
kwest ay lah rah-**gah**-tsa
that's the girl

scusi
skoo-see
Excuse me

signorina, scusi scusi! Sono molto, molto spiacente!
  seen-yor-**een**-ah, **scoo**-see **scoo**-see! **soh**-noh **mohl**-toh, **mohl**-toh spee-ah-**chen**-tay!
Excuse me, Miss, I'm very, very sorry!

Si, si, andando a Ravello, ho detto
see, see, ahn-**dahn**-doh ah rah-**vel**-loh, oh **day**-toh
yes, yes, we're going to Ravello, I told you

Tortellini al Pomodoro
tor-tel-**lee**-nee ahl poh-moh-**dor**-oh
cheese pockets filled pasta with a tomato sauce

Tuttomondo
too-toh-**mon**-doh
worldwide (whole world)

EXCERPT FROM NERO GOES TO ROME

CHAPTER 24

CAROLINE'S STORY

Inside the church, the only light came from a series of arched windows high up in the walls. Columns surrounded the empty circular interior and cast spooky shadows on the smooth marble floor. Gianni remained still for a moment, listening – so did Nero. There wasn't a sound, unless you counted our breathing. He turned on his flashlight. In its beam, the gold bracelet around my wrist glittered. It suddenly seemed very, very heavy.

Nero and I followed Gianni to the far side of the church, where he eased behind a column and knelt by a large wooden trapdoor in the floor, which had a rusted iron ring attached.

"Help me," he whispered. We tugged at the ring, the heavy trapdoor opened and Gianni aimed his flashlight into the darkness. Beneath the trapdoor was a spiral staircase cut into the rock.

"This leads down to the Boschetti vault," he said. Although he was whispering, his voice echoed off the walls around us. "Below the vault are the catacombs."

The very word made me shiver. One of the few things that stuck in my head from Miss Moreno's history class was how the early Christians buried their dead in the catacombs. I even remembered Didi's disgusted, "How gross is *that*?" Little did she know that one day she'd find out first-hand.

"There are some two miles of passageways under this church according to my calculations."

"Two miles!" I was unable to keep my voice from trembling.

"That's just the area I surveyed. There might be another three miles of undiscovered passages down there."

"Uh – how far down there?"

"Only about sixty feet." He started down the worn stone steps. I stayed where I was – *sixty feet*!

"Come on!" he whispered urgently. I took a few cautious steps down into the blackness. Gianni wouldn't let up. "Of course, only about seventy per cent of all the catacombs in Rome have been opened and explored. It's believed that the total length of the network is something like five hundred miles."

We continued down the slippery stone steps, worn smooth by centuries of pilgrims' feet until I was giddy from the spiral. Once in a while, Nero paused at a broken step and uttered a tiny sound, as if to warn us.

After we'd descended about thirty feet, we came to a landing just big enough for the three of us. A wooden door with a rusted iron latch was open a crack. Gianni lowered the beam and there on the floor was a heavy lock – twisted and broken.

I knew from his expression that the lock hadn't been broken the last time he was here. He pushed gently at the door. More stairs!

At the bottom of the steps was a large vaulted room carved into the rock. Gianni shone the light around the walls, which were lined with marble tablets inscribed in Latin.

"The Boschetti family tombs," he explained in a whisper. *Thanks a lot,* I thought, *I really needed to know that.* I shivered. It was very, *very* cold. Gianni buttoned his jacket up over the coil of rope, and he looked strangely bulky in the half-light.

He referred once again to his map, then edged behind a large jutting tombstone. He ran his fingers along the grooves separating the marble slabs on the wall, then –

"Yes!"

A narrow section of the wall moved back with a grating sound. It was a doorway and beyond it was total – and I mean *total* – darkness. Even Nero seemed reluctant to enter. I certainly was – and my reluctance turned to downright terror when Gianni announced in a triumphant whisper, "The Catacombs of Santa Maria."

He headed into the blackness. I followed. A long passageway stretched ahead of us, just wide enough for two people and a dog and we walked its length cautiously. At last it opened out into a wider chamber. On the far side, we were faced with not one archway, but four! And all of them pitch black.

"We need the North Passage," Gianni said.

"How do we know which that is?" I whispered.

"With this." From his pocket he produced a compass on a long loop of cord. "Take it."

I put the cord round my neck and held the compass out so Gianni could examine it with the flashlight. I admit I was impressed with his foresight.

"Keep it steady," he whispered. "I can't read it with you shaking it around like that." *No more than you're shaking the flashlight around*, I thought. But I was glad he was nervous too – it would keep us both on our toes. After some hesitation Gianni pointed to a very narrow archway that looked even darker than the others, if that was possible.

"I *think* that's it." He took Didi's shoe out of his pocket and held it out to Nero, who inspected it with a series of rapid sniffs. "What do you say Nero?"

Nero turned his attention to the passages before us, then walked towards the tunnel that Gianni had indicated. We followed.

"Stay close," Gianni said. "People have been known to get lost in the catacombs, never to be seen again."

That did it. I grabbed his jacket and stayed so close I trod on his heels.

The passage was so narrow I could touch both sides of it easily, and at one point I heard Gianni curse softly as he hit his head on the ceiling. We hadn't gone far when we started down a steep slope.

"*Attenzione!*" he whispered and grabbed my arm. We were at the top of a flight of steep narrow steps cut directly into rock.

"Are you sure this is right?"

"I think so," he whispered. Again we looked to Nero, who started off gingerly down the steps.

The going was slow because the steps were so uneven, and every so often one was missing. Several times I slipped and almost fell on top of Gianni. We were a long way underground now and I was seized with claustrophobia. I took a couple of deep breaths, but the dank, earthy air did little to revive me.

Suddenly Nero stopped and let out a low growl. Gianni clicked off the flashlight.

There was a faint glow coming from somewhere ahead of us. Gianni nudged me and put a finger to his lips. What did he think I was going to do – burst into song?

Moving quietly now, we reached the bottom of the steps and came into a wide cavern. At its centre was a deep circular pit of some kind – it must've been about fifteen feet wide. The light was coming from deep inside it.

Nero crouched down close to the floor and crept forward one paw at a time. Motioning me to stay where I was, Gianni followed him to the edge of the pit. He turned and beckoned to me to join him, indicating that I should keep my head low.

As I moved cautiously forward, a blood-curdling scream ripped through the stale air and echoed round the vaults and passageways.

It was Didi.

Made in the USA
Lexington, KY
19 March 2012